THE BIG DROP *HOMECOMING*
Ryan Gattis

A Johnny Ban Book

Copyright © 2013 by Ryan Gattis

ISBN-13: 978-0615699134
ISBN-10: 0615699138

Edited by Carmen Harbour
Artwork by Mark Smith

Printed in the U.S.A.

BLACK HILL PRESS
Contemporary American Novellas
blackhillpress.com

Black Hill Press is a publishing collective founded on collaboration. Our growing family of writers and artists are dedicated to the novella—a distinctive, often overlooked literary form that offers the focus of a short story and the scope of a novel. We believe a great story is never defined by its length.

Annually, our independent press produces four quarterly collections of Contemporary American Novellas. Books are available in both print and digital formats, online and in your local bookstore, library, museum, university gift shop, and selected specialty accounts. Discounts are available for book clubs and teachers.

This book would not have been possible without the aid, understanding, insight, and skill of the following people: Kevin Staniec, Janet Kim, Pam Gattis, Bob Gattis, Annazell Gattis, Brandon Gattis, Marisa Roemer, David Mitchell, Paul Paulson, J.D. Lawrence, Mark Smith, Carmen Harbour, Tom Broderick, Ryan Ramirez, Ryan Hammill, Sean Haeseler, Bill Peace, Angie Reynoso, CharLee Williams, The Takemoto Family, Rimban Hiroshi Abiko, George K. Takahashi, and Ken. Thank you all. I simply couldn't have done it without you.

THE BIG DROP

Johnny Ban wasn't himself—hadn't been for some time. He had left Osaka a thirty-two-year-old, but he felt sure the last few days had aged him to eighty. His joints hurt and he was forgetting things, important things, like his seizure medication.

Leaving Los Angeles wouldn't cure any of it, but it would help. The city of his birth had beaten him down so badly he was certain he had shrunk. He hadn't, of course. He just found it a little harder to stand up straight.

He still was five foot nine. Still had the same thick-chested frame, brawler's shoulders, and the thin paunch to go with both. He still had the scars.

He would always have those scars—four ragged pits on his left cheek. Four burgundy bottle-mouths that looked as if a panther had put its claws in, twisted, and pulled out four corks at the same time.

In the king-size bed, propped up between a Georgian headboard and a mess of high-thread-count sheets, Johnny Ban ran a hand down his face. His fingers didn't want to stop trembling.

He knew he was in Ayaki Hayami's house. In the upstairs master bedroom.

The lone light in the place came through the bathroom door twenty feet away. It slanted a gold rectangle on the far wall, spotlighting semi-opaque shadows of water dancing over bad wallpaper. It was flooded inside that bathroom, and it was only getting worse.

Behind the glowing door, the toilet had gone to pieces. Its plumbing had been sheared off at the wall. The water hadn't been turned off, and as a result, the spewing pipes made it sound like a broken fountain in there, like fierce raindrops hitting the surface of a pond.

Johnny shivered.

Out of habit, he tapped still-trembling fingers on his right hip pocket, on the place his medicine bottle had always been, but the familiar rattle wasn't there, and that knowledge made it hard to breathe.

Because in Johnny's world, there were consequences for forgetfulness. Already, he could feel it coming, could feel it breathing frost onto his skin. Either the room had grown lungs or the seizure was telling him it was close, almost there, ready to make him disappear.

The big drop, he called it.

That was how it felt when it came: like the world was flat, like he could get knocked clear off the edge of it and plunge into a swirling patch of deep space.

But the big drop was a process. And it was coming all right. It promised that much. Not now, but soon.

Johnny knew it too well. It would arrive slowly, coldly, whispering icicles over his skin before stealing his ability to speak or move. His tongue would seize up then, and the rest of his muscles would domino.

That's when the electricity would pay a visit. It was considerate that way, because when he couldn't move, couldn't defend himself, it would tear through his nerves like he'd stuck a fork in a live socket, and when it was done playing with him, when it had crisped him good, his field of vision would narrow to a single point, blackening everything around him, as if his entire world had jammed itself into an elevator above his head, and then, when the cord got cut, it all landed on his skull.

He didn't have much time. Two minutes, maybe three.

The nightstand phone coughed up a dial tone. Johnny put Rooney's number in. He had it memorized by now. The line on the other side didn't even ring. It just clicked.

"Central Homicide Unit. Rooney speaking."

"I found her, Detective."

"Found who?"

Johnny touched the pressure dressing on his thigh. His hand came back bloody. Not too bloody, but bloody enough to worry. One red finger and one red thumb. He looked at his fingertips, willed them to stop trembling, and said the name he didn't think he could say, "Emi."

"You mean Emi Sato?"

Johnny eyed the bathroom door.

"I couldn't leave her in there. I had to move her to the bed." He knew he sounded crazy, but his tongue was going now, was making its last stand. "All that water isn't good for you."

Rooney covered the phone, whispered something to a colleague before coming back on. "Is she dead, Ban?"

It took Johnny a long time to answer.

"Yes," he finally said.

"Did you kill her?"

Johnny couldn't look at the lumpy line of Emi Sato's form buried under heaped sheets. Instead, he stared at a scar shaped like a minnow on her protruding forearm.

"Maybe."

"Where are you?"

"Hollywood."

"Were you in that goddamn guerrilla shootout?" Rooney pronounced each syllable like he meant to strangle Johnny through the phone. "You better hold this line, Ban. We're tracing it. And if you're there..."

"Everybody plays a role in this town." Johnny cradled Emi's arm close to his chest. "Every single person is the best actor you ever saw."

"You're not telling me anything new," Rooney let his last word dangle before shotgunning Johnny with a question they both knew was coming, "are you, *Kenji*?"

A slow, sad grin split Johnny's face. He hated that frog and that name. Hated him almost as much as the thick frost gathering on his cheeks. On his neck. Wrapping itself around his tongue.

"You got me, Detective," he said, laying his head back against the pillow. His words were slurring, falling apart as he spoke them. "I'm... going away... now."

Rooney screamed something, demanded an answer. But Johnny didn't have one. He couldn't move a muscle.

For him, the earth was already flat. The big drop had seen to that, and it was pushing him over the edge, out into space, into the merry-go-round of stars, as a police battering ram popped the front door's hinges and a seizure gripped Johnny, turning his whole body into a catcher's mitt for lightning.

CINEMA ALLEY

It all started about a week ago, in Osaka. From the beginning, the whole thing was Kenji's fault. *Kaeru* Kenji. Kenji the Frog. He lit the fuse, did it on purpose.

He came by the nickname honestly. In every possible way, Kenji Asada had a face like a frog. Where his forehead should've been, a rounded rise sat crowned with two far-flung eyes. His chin had battled his neck long ago and lost, and ever since, his throat had been massing for a push toward his nose, which was little more than a bump hosting parenthetical slits.

Of course, Kenji tried to make up for this deficiency by wearing colorful vests that he paired with earth-toned suits and plaid neckerchiefs. It was all calculated to drag attention from his face.

It never worked. Everyone who ever saw the man in the flesh got a visceral reaction at first glimpse. Everyone. Man, woman, and child.

Johnny too.

It was barely morning, with navy blue pox-dots breaking out across the summer night sky, when Johnny Ban first ducked into a ware-filled alley that hadn't been there on his first trip through earlier in the evening.

Osaka's Cinema Alley wasn't an alley at all. It was a traveling marketplace, one that moved to avoid the law. A makeshift cockroach of a market, the sixteen stalls crept around the Doutonburi—the canal district that connected the north and south branches of the Yohori River—and set up shop wherever it found space, mostly in alleyways that snaked between adjoining yakuza properties.

Vendors in this tiny quarter spoke a few words of Japanese and little else. It didn't take much to communicate that movies scheduled for release next month were already out on DVD, hanging from see-through plastic curtains. You looked, you wanted, you bought—didn't get simpler than that.

To Johnny, the whole place smelled like body odor, foreign cigarettes, and newly pressed plastic, but that didn't bother him. Not that night. For once, he was in a good mood.

He tapped his hip pockets in alternating fashion. One rattled with his pills, one jingled with his keys. Habit. He couldn't take six steps otherwise. It was a way not to forget. A way to stay normal.

Somewhere behind his eyes a headache brewed, and his legs hadn't forgiven him for sitting through a double bill of old and new, Joseph L. Mankiewicz's *Somewhere in the Night* alongside Ben Silver's debut flick, *Don't Run*, at the Super Harmony Theatre. Johnny liked Silver. He'd come a long way from crime flicks to big budget art stuff that cast locals as extras and gobbled annual awards like pigs clear slop.

Johnny loved movies, always had. If he had a vice, maybe that was it. That, or pining badly for a girl that had disappeared without a trace sixteen years ago. One of the two.

The only reason Johnny's legs weren't on strike that night was because he'd had a few whiskey sours at the dirtiest international bar this side of Thailand, The Blue Dahlia. He could drink there and not be bothered, not be asked why half his face looked like a panther tried to dig it out and wear it as a headdress. He liked that.

He liked it so much he didn't pay attention to where he was going, or who was following.

The first kick caught Johnny flush in the back of his right knee. He stumbled forward, slapping asphalt with open palms to keep himself up. Before he could stand, he took a shot to the ribs. A boot heel careened off his hip just after.

That did it. Johnny went down like a figure skater misjudging his landing. The alley floor punched him with a cocktail of motor oil and dog spray as dirty asphalt barked his knees, his chin. His hands came back graveled, bleeding, stinging like a hive of hornets had used them for target practice.

Some guys stay down until they get let up, and then they stay down the rest of their lives. They walk around flat inside ever after, like ruined soufflés.

Johnny Ban wasn't that guy.

In fact, you could say that was Johnny's number one problem: he always got back up.

"You a cripple, Ban?"

His attacker wanted to know.

Johnny spun on his bad leg. He was in luck—it held him. Slinging a glance at a frog-faced little man in a brown tweed suit and a fluorescent-orange vest that gleamed like an open wound, he laughed at what he saw.

He shouldn't have.

A knife leapt to Kenji's fist. Its blade caught neon, angled itself at Johnny. The metal went pink, then red. This wasn't a knife—it was a machete's younger brother.

Johnny boomeranged his gaze around the alley: up the narrow passage, then back the way he'd come. It didn't return with good news. The vendors had all lined up like this was free entertainment. Mouths hung loose on their hinges. Hungry eyes refused to blink.

"What the hell is this about?" Johnny swiped grit from his burning palms. No one could forget that face. Not even him.

He didn't get a response. Instead, the knife swung low. The air where Johnny had been standing parted audibly and rolled back in two fast swirls.

"Not so slow!" The frog's throat bulged as he patted his belly. "Why tap your pockets? Something there going to save you?"

Johnny rattled his pocket just to show Kenji he could. Then, he did it once more because he had to.

The knife darted his way, but Johnny wasn't there. It was a good dodge. Not the best. It would've been better if it hadn't sandwiched him in a stall. Johnny took a step and broke two DVD cases laid out on a blanket. Behind him, someone groaned.

Kenji didn't swing again, he stabbed, so Johnny sidestepped and his left leg let him. He shifted his weight, threw a fast right jab at Kenji's knife-hand as it slid by. He aimed for the wrist.

He missed.

Johnny's fist caught Kenji's elbow at the crease, caving in the Frog's extended arm like he'd popped the safety catch on a stepladder, crashing the thing from ninety degrees to forty-five in half a heartbeat. Johnny caught the knife-hand with his frantic left, and bent it back. Right into its owner.

His iffy left leg gave in then, pitching him sideways—dragging Kenji down with him right onto the cutting edge, extinguishing every last inch of its neon glow with a wet belly thump on the asphalt.

The frog spasmed as he lurched over onto his chest, grunting only once, like a popped balloon. Veins jumped to attention on his face, and black-and-white space shuttle eyes tried to liftoff in his sockets. His mouth tried a scream on for size, but his lungs wanted no part of it.

There was something unreal about the way Kenji gasped and stopped, and gasped again. About the way his blood soaked Johnny from shoes to waist so fast that it hardly seemed like blood at all.

But Johnny had seen too many movies. Kenji's plasma surged out in thick-black tongues on the alley floor, licking through gravel divots like a lake overflowing its banks. And he wasn't breathing. Not one gulp.

Around them, vendors speed-stuffed their wares into sacks, collapsed shelves, unplugged lights and televisions, shoved mashed-full crates onto dolly-carts.

To Johnny, their exodus felt like a day. It must have been seconds.

He was still sitting upright in the alley, half-dazed and wheezing, when two men with arms bigger than their thighs ragdolled him out of Kenji's blood puddle, smashed a canvas hood down over his head, threw him in the trunk of a moving car, and slammed it closed.

UNDERWORLD

Johnny felt the basement before he saw it. Newspapers crinkled under his knees as two rough pairs of hands forced him to kneel, then bow, then sit straight.

Like a ripped band-aid, his hood left his head in one harsh pull. A gun replaced it, its barrel divotting his right temple until it left a mouth-mark and then quit. His two captors stayed behind him. There was no mistaking their looming.

The wooziness he had felt in the alley had all but gone. He was clear, clear enough to be terrified. He had taken a good beating on the way in. A careful one. One that ignored his face and ribs and concentrated on soft spots. His thighs. His arms. His stomach. A net-like ache spread over his body now, caught him up whole.

No bigger than a shed, the room was tatamied wall-to-wall and purposely underlit. The place smelled of wet cat food and wetter cats, but Johnny didn't put two and two together until furry bodies brushed against him in the dark.

There must've been nine or ten of them wriggling around the tiny room, mewling in groups like competing feline choirs.

"We know who you are," a voice said.

Funny, Johnny thought, the guy with the knife did too.

"Call me Oni." The voice came from a man standing in front of him.

His name meant demon, but he sure didn't look like one. He was track-suited and sixty-ish, sporting a haircut like a black cap on a milk bottle. He had large bony knees that bulged against too-tight nylon as he leaned down to pour food into a trough. Cats cut their singing and bolted to the sound.

"Okay," Johnny mumbled. It was less a reply than to make sure his jaw still worked. It did, only it acted like newly molded gelatin just learning how to wobble.

"We have a problem," Oni said.

A fist buried itself so deeply in Johnny's left kidney that he felt it in his toenails. He couldn't stifle a moan as he pitched forward and the newspaper rushed up to meet him. The headline was familiar: *American Businessman Gunned Down in Umeda*.

Johnny knew this story. Everybody did. The CEO of a company called R4 had been shot. The Romanized letter and number combination drew Johnny's gaze amongst the sea of Japanese characters. This paper was six days old.

The same rough hands returned him to his knees.

"You see, the man you killed, Kenji Asada, was yakuza, and regardless of how you may feel about our milieu, we have rules." Oni spread his hands to show Johnny that it was out of his control. "How Kenji died is of no consequence, but I have one dead boy, which means you have a debt. Payable two ways, of course."

So it wouldn't feel left out, Johnny's right kidney caught a boot. As he fell, the picture of the dead American CEO jumped up and met him. *Edward Galt*, the too-big caption said. The blow brought tears to Johnny's eyes and when they fell, Galt's big chin wobbled and went wet in a circle. Through clenched teeth, Johnny exhaled long and slow.

No hands picked him up this time. He had to struggle to his knees himself.

"The first is too distasteful to mention, but the second may intrigue you. You see, Asada was booked on a morning flight to Los Angeles. He was to inform us of the location of a very valuable item. And seeing as how you have a background in English, First Sergeant..."

Background. It was Oni's understated way of saying he knew Johnny had been a translator in the Japanese Ground Self-Defense Forces, and that despite Johnny's medical status, he still saw him as valuable, retired or not.

When no blow came, Johnny blinked hard. He wiped his cheeks on his shoulders. Left, then right. He tapped his left front pocket to hear the soft rattle of his seizure medication, and he tapped his right, to feel the teeth of his apartment keys.

So long as Ban could still speak English, he could keep breathing. That was what the word background meant when Oni said it. It also meant that if Johnny Ban had any doubts about being set up, he sure as hell didn't now.

"She was last seen in Little Tokyo. Give him a list."

A sheet of paper dropped into Johnny's lap. The thing was written in English, and had three different establishments on it. Johnny ran it down.

KARAOKE WEEKEND
NISHI TEMPLE
THE SOFT SPOT

"After being seen in each of these places, she pulled the slickest of disappearing acts." Oni leaned forward, accentuating the words with his hands. "Now, we have tried various ways of drawing her out, but to no avail."

"Just find her? Nothing else?"

Oni nodded. It was a long, gray nod—the kind that could mean yes and no at the same time.

"And if I fail?"

The gun reacquainted itself with Johnny's head.

"You have eight days. Find her and you have no debt. We will pay your expenses, of course."

A plane ticket hit the newspaper in front of him. A brick of bills followed it, along with an international phone that a brown cat couldn't resist batting.

"The hotel is booked for Asada. So is the plane ticket. The phone dials one number. Mine. Call anytime."

Johnny caught the drift. "So I need to be Kenji."

A board slapped the back of his head, and a camera he hadn't seen went flash in his face. Johnny blinked hard as dots sparred in his peripheral vision. The careful beating made sense now. They had been preserving his looks.

"America fingerprints aliens." Johnny knew it wasn't much, but it was something. "They will know the difference."

"Asada never left," Oni assured him, "and you have never been fingerprinted there either."

"G.S.D. might still have mine on file."

"Even if they wanted to, America lacks the capability to check the files of every government and military organization in the world, much less those of its allies." Oni slid a photo across the newspaper. "Her name is Emi."

This item wasn't much to look at, not for folks who found thin lips and skin the texture of boiled wallpaper attractive. For everyone else, she was a sloe-eyed Venus with her hair up, and she was smiling like her face would fall to pieces if she didn't.

"Tasteful lighting," Johnny said.

When Oni's lips ran away from his teeth, it triggered a slow shiver down Johnny's back. The man must have thought it was a smile, his own special brand.

"With any luck, Johnny," Oni's voice grated over the words, "you will be our catnip."

Johnny didn't respond. He was too busy studying the white slash of light across the girl's face in the picture.

It loved her too-big eyes and her nose, but it ignored parts of her face too. Her ears. Her hairline. Part of her cheek. These lay deep in shadow.

It was skillful editing. Editing with tilted lights, but editing nonetheless. Anyone who had never seen her in person would think it artistic, striking even. Wouldn't even wonder what that darkness hid.

But Johnny knew.

He would know that face anywhere.

Deep down, his guts stomped a war dance in nine-eight time. And he let them because they knew her full name was Emi Sato.

And they knew Johnny hadn't seen her since the day she disappeared. And they knew that because they had burned for her
every day since.

EMI SATO

Emi Sato had always been a jawbreaker. Ever since she was a little girl, she had a candy coating and a hard little center, not the kind people are born with, but the kind that's made. The kind that only goes one of two ways once it gets crushed together by years of hurtful thises and hateful thats, after stored-up words and painful deeds have been fired by a brainpan kiln until it congeals into a round, hard thing—either a pearl, or a bullet—and the outside's just a shell.

Her family had lived on a hill outside Osaka, Johnny remembered that much. But where it was exactly, or how to get back to it, he didn't know. He only remembered the whiskered asphalt slope and the tall Western house atop it, the two-story blue one garlanded with ash trees that peered down on its neighbors.

He had knocked on that oaken front door the last day he ever saw her. She had been gone from school all week, serving yet another suspension for fighting someone who called her Yin-Yang Girl or Yogurt Face.

But when she opened the door that day, she didn't tell him she would be disappearing that very night. She didn't tell him she would leave no trace, or that she would abandon a tight-lipped family, and a boy named Johnny wondering if it was his fault that she had gone.

Instead, Emi Sato smiled. She hid one arm behind her back, grinned wide, and said, "I want to show you something!"

That was Johnny's cue to put quick hands in his pockets. He would do anything for that face, and he didn't want her knowing it.

There was nothing like her skin.

Her two-tone face looked like a map, he thought. Her ears sat on pink islands shaped like mirrored images of Antarctica. An archipelago of smaller spots chin-strapped her white jawline. Her pale nose was a glacier, and beneath everything, the structure was perfect: high cheekbones, a chin with just the right amount of sharpness, and bright wide eyes. She was a Venus with vitiligo, and she had hated her skin spots every second of her life.

He asked if her parents were home and set off Emi's rich-girl-snicker, the one that only flowed when she was queen of the palace. Still smiling, she took his hand.

Sure, the Satos had money and plenty of it. Mr. Sato wore tailored gray suits and worked for politicians. He did things, but what those things were, and where the money came from, nobody knew. More importantly, nobody asked. Johnny certainly never thought to. It simply was.

Scents of wood wax and steamed rice hit Johnny as Emi swept him past the dining table and the girl hunched over a textbook there. He locked eyes with her little sister.

Stern and studious, Hana had perfect, one-toned skin, but only half her sister's beauty. Her glasses sat haphazardly on her average little forehead, tangled in oily hair.

Upstairs, Emi's room had changed. The laces and reds of last year were extinct. Her half-open closet was now blacker than the mouths of Heian-era court ladies who painted high eyebrows on their foreheads and wrote poems all day.

She flopped on the bed chest-first and patted the comforter beside her. He folded his arms and leaned against her desk instead. It took all his strength not to join her immediately.

She shrugged and sat up, fussing with a cuff.

"Now my skin does what I tell it to," Emi said.

She tugged the shirtsleeve up from her wrist and over her forearm, revealing a hooked scar along her elbow. Thin as a toothpick and raised like a sticky minnow lying dead on her skin, it shared the healthy pinkness of her ears.

"It dances too," she said, and giggled. When she flexed, it jerked like a puppet.

"And it can be explained away," she said, tapping her teeth. "I think... a bicycling accident caused this. I guess I fell on some glass."

Johnny moved to the bed, squeaking its springs as he settled in. He felt awkward and small as he ran a finger down the pink island that owned her left ear.

Emi pouted. "Why touch it?"

"Because I like to," he said.

"I show you something great," she snapped, "and you focus on my *flaws*."

"Maybe because they are beautiful." His finger surfed the white ocean to her chin, dropped in on the curl of her collarbone. "Not flaws."

He was waiting to be told no, to be told to stop, but the rebuke never came, so his fingertip dodged the blotted pigmentation around her hairline and found its way to the paleness at the nape of her neck, the kind that mimicked a powdered apprentice geisha's, only permanent, only done by nature's own hand.

"You just like it," she continued, "because you think I look on the outside how you look on the inside."

She meant she was white and pink, two different colors together, but separate. Unmeshable. It was nothing she hadn't said before. It was one of her favorite things to chuck at him. But the way she said it stopped Johnny's finger. For his classmates and for his mother's friends, his Americanness cancelled out his Japaneseness. He was only *hafu* to them. Half. Two disconnected parts that didn't add up to a whole anything.

But together, he and Emi were something. Two misfits finding a fit. His fingertip started up again, running marathons around her island coasts and promontories then, even to her bruises. Storm clouds and layered yellow blankets blobbed her ribs and thighs. She didn't flinch.

He put his knuckle scars up against her elbow, lifted his shirt and gauged the Australia-shaped bruise of his own, the one where he had caught a bat with his ribs. The one where he had learned bullies never go away when you beat them, they just hit you from behind next time. He moved to pull his shirt down, but she pushed his weight out from under him and rolled on top, pinning his shoulders.

When she brought her face close to Johnny's, it seemed to him she was bullying everyone who ever bullied her. He was a prone scapegoat, a sacrifice, and she kissed him like most women slap. Fierce, quick. Shocked by her velocity, her own raw strength.

He took it. Anything was worth it to be with Emi. It didn't matter that it scared him, he liked it, and he didn't care if she knew it.

One room away, Hana held her breath as she slung black hair back behind an ear and pressed her whole body to the shared wall, to listen.

L.A.

When Johnny's plane landed in Los Angeles, he couldn't shake a certain adolescent anxiety, a clumsy little lead-footed feeling that stomped around in his chest. Emi is here, it whispered. He just had to find her and ask her to dance. But he had to get to Kenji's hotel first. He had to call Oni before he went out looking. That was the deal.

His fingerprints hadn't brought up any red flags at Customs. For all he knew, they had been assigned to Kenji's passport in the U.S. database and that was that. It was smooth sailing through baggage claim. Just a 'Nothing to Declare' lane, a stamped landing card, and an awed aside from a guard that Johnny spoke such good English and to enjoy his California vacation.

Johnny massaged his kidneys, nodded, grabbed his bag. He had pissed blood over the Pacific, and he would do it again on dry land, but that couldn't be helped now.

From the airport to the blue bus and out into the Union Station terminal with its ceiling like an inverted book spine with chandelier piercings, Johnny Ban tapped his pockets. The breast of his only good suit rattlesnaked under his fingers as his pills made like maracas.

The bomb had made him into this, a habitual pocket-tapper. Now, it was the only way to make sure he wasn't forgetting anything.

So he tapped his pills again, and his list and cash on his left hip, and the phone and passport and Emi's picture on his right. His fingers remembered better than his brain did. His last doctor had said that.

Now this tapping was the only thing keeping Johnny on an even keel. That, and the medication. Concepts, names, some faces, all remained clear in his brain—mostly clear—hazed on the edges maybe, but with clear middles, like looking down a kaleidoscope barrel.

The little things though—remembering to wash his hair in the shower, to put on socks, to pour water into the rice cooker before flipping the switch, to pocket his keys and his wallet—had become hourly disasters. So, as advised, he'd built patterns, and he used them to glue his life back together.

A few pairs of eyes flicked to him as he walked the terminal, tapping. Johnny had long grown used to eyes following him. They had done it his whole life: diagnosed his ethnicity and found it deficient.

In Osaka, he wasn't Japanese enough. He wasn't anything until he joined the Ground Self-Defense Forces, only then was his halfness good for something. It was a skill. A specialization. Only then did he matter.

But all that became secondary when the bomb tore half his face off. Questioning eyes became distrustful eyes, fearful eyes that thought him criminal, violent.

And here, in a chocolate-hued, high-beamed cathedral that smelled of bagels and burnt coffee, these American eyes didn't linger on his panther marks, and that feeling was new to Johnny, both strange and good at the same time.

Sure, one or two looked. Most didn't. What was more, they didn't weigh him up, they simply acknowledged and ticked away. Some folks even nodded. One smiled.

Johnny looked away. He dragged his eyes to a copper-worked clock hanging over a courtyard doorway. He surveyed travelers, commuters, people killing time. It wasn't quite what he expected of the America he had read about in the news or seen on television.

None were morbidly obese. Two were a little fat, sure, but not ready to be put out to pasture. Of those who sat, most read books, or slept with their heads lolled, or spoke quietly in groups of two or three.

Within minutes he had seen ten, a dozen mixed race people parading down the tiled center aisle toward the trains. A trio of caramel children with kinked blond hair strolled by in a pack, their heads held high.

A minute later, he saw a girl like him, a beanpole *hafu*, one with a freckled face and chunky glasses that framed Asian eyes. The oddest feeling struck him then. He wanted to hug her, to tell her his own story, to share.

He didn't. Instead, he walked out into the gauzy sort of morning light that California has a patent on. He skipped the taxis and headed south on foot. It was only four and a half blocks to the hotel.

He fought sunglasses out of his pocket and breathed in Los Angeles, the blue air with an earthbound beige ring around it, the Sierras he could barely see the hips of, the skyscrapers of the downtown area rising on his right like a gemmed gauntlet punching straight up out of the ground.

It was horizontal, this city. Not like Japan. Her big cities were vertical. Unviewable from the streets. Perspective just wasn't possible from ground level there. Here, it was mandatory.

Alameda Street took him over the morning parking lot that was the 101 Freeway. He kept his feet to the sidewalk and clamped his eyes on Little Tokyo, three blocks down.

It had been home for his first nine years, and now he couldn't look at it without seeing a few layers of the past. He had his mother — rest her soul — to thank for that. To her, Little Tokyo was always an iceberg: a cool, calm surface masking a mountain of pain beneath. But maybe that was to be expected of a place where both Japanese and American citizens were rounded up, put on buses, and sent to concentration camps by their own government. She used to say Executive Order 9066 emptied more houses than a plague would have.

When she was alive, his mother had been after him to leave a legacy in honor of those that had come before, those that had suffered. And here Johnny was, thirty-two years old, with nothing to leave behind. Not unless you counted him donating a chunk of his skull to the desert, just outside the Suq al Masgoof in Samawah, Iraq.

Johnny Ban hadn't done much in his life, but he knew what an IED felt like. And he knew brain injuries inside and out.

Johnny swept fingers from his scars to his right temple. That small bit of bone hadn't forgotten what a gun muzzle felt like. And it wouldn't any time soon. But it was a funny thing about being blown-up, and Johnny knew this deeper than his scars, you get a feeling like nothing that bad can ever happen again, but if it did—so be it.

He had a long time to think while on Kenji's flight, and Johnny had come to one conclusion about the whole thing. He was actually thankful for Oni's transparent setup, thankful because it had dropped a parcel of purpose on his doorstep. Thankful because he had almost forgotten what that felt like.

But if Oni thought Johnny Ban was going along because of one little pistol-kiss to the head and a threat, then he needed to guess again.

Those weren't the kinds of things that scared a man who had been through three brain surgeries, a month in rehab, and thirteen months in therapy.

Johnny was in America for Emi Sato, and only for Emi Sato. To find out why she left the first time. To find out why she had been gone all these years. No other reason.

Well, maybe just one.

LITTLE TOKYO

Johnny was thinking about whether he still loved Emi, or could still love Emi after all these years not seeing her, when he cut the corner onto East 1st Street and kept on walking until he hit Central. It was there that his gaze jumped to a helicopter chopping the sky above City Hall wearing its ziggurat hat, before landing on San Pedro Street a block down.

The low row of buildings between looked like brick-headed schoolchildren sitting on their knees. Kenji's hotel was the whitest pile halfway down the row, the one with a jag of exposed pipe and a runny nose.

All along the sidewalk, fake trees masked parking meters, hiding their bulbous heads with brown plasticine trunks. Their shade cut leaf-shapes onto four classic sedans shining like new pennies along the curb.

Churning over and around this scene, careful not to touch bumpers or lean on trees, was a tightly packed crowd, two hundred strong. Men, women, and children allowed themselves to be herded by people waving clipboards. Johnny couldn't help scanning the crowd for Emi's face, and didn't see it. Not that it was ever likely.

He did learn, however, that there was only one clear route to the hotel: through.

He hadn't gone twenty feet before he hit a knot so thick it couldn't be untied without twisting a few arms. So he stopped. Beside him, he saw a Japanese face and spoke Japanese to it. It was a mistake.

"Excuse me," he said to a fifty-ish woman with a face as round as a timpani drum, "but what is all this?"

"Wow," the woman spoke directly to his scars, her voice heavy with awe. "Your Japanese is wonderful."

He asked again in English, sheepishly.

Her drum tightened. She made a face like he was playing a joke on her, and it wasn't funny.

"*Impermanence,*" she said, gauging his reaction.

"I'm afraid I don't understand what that means."

"But you're dressed for it." Her eyebrows dropped down on her eyes as she indicated Johnny's suit with an extended pinkie. "And you're here..."

"I'm just going to my hotel." Johnny nodded toward his snot-nosed accommodations.

She didn't believe him, and maybe his scars had something to do with that, because she eyed them like they were a communicable disease.

"It's our movie," she said softly. "They're shooting a crowd scene today."

Out of pure cinephilic curiosity, Johnny asked who the director was.

Her unbudgeable eyes kept on his scars. She spoke to them more than him. "Ben Silver," she said.

Johnny nodded his thanks to the woman and thought of how he had seen Silver's first movie only a few hours ago in Osaka, and how it felt like longer, like weeks. But it felt strange too, like maybe he was meant to be here. Right now.

A heavyset worker with a forehead bigger than her face waded toward them, parting the crowd into two separate seas. She got within two feet of Johnny and stopped to sling a finger at him. The thick digit arrowed for his scars, but Johnny shrugged it off.

"They didn't give you an umbrella?" The woman had enough skull to dole out transplants and still have some left over. "We need men up higher on the street. And, buddy, all day is something I don't got."

If higher up on the street meant closer to his hotel, Johnny was for it. Forehead nodded that it was, so he followed her up through the crowd.

IMPERMANENCE

When Johnny slid out of the mob and had enough room to breathe without bouncing off somebody, he looked down 1st, at a parking lot packed with white trailers. Across from it stood a dark-wooded shopping center roofed in blue tile, one that wrapped itself around a red *yagura*, a six-legged fire tower.

On this block, only the Miyako Hotel stood taller, and carts stocked to their hinges with film gear littered the sidewalk at its ankles. An unmanned crane, one with a camera perched atop its arm, sat dead in the middle of 1st Street, straddling the yellow line.

Next to it was an antique hearse with two chatting actors seated on its back bumper. Johnny didn't recognize them, but they had Japanese faces. Not Korean. Not Malaysian. Yamato faces. Faces like Emi's—almost.

Johnny had a chance to break away, but he didn't take it. He had always wondered how movies were made, and it didn't help that his jetlag had been working on him, weighing his feet down, fuzzing his brain up, making it easier for people to push him this way and that.

Johnny let himself get shuttled into a line that provided him with an overcoat, a dusty fedora that was a size too big, and a battered umbrella. Nobody said anything about his beat-up leather suitcase. Forehead just told him to stand with a group of similarly dressed cattle under a suspended stretch of pipe with sprinklers all down its length.

Cattle. That was the word she used.

Before long, a man in a white shirt, jean shorts, and hiking boots organized them into lines on the curb of 1st. He looked more like a wrestler than a filmmaker, the way he checked costumes, or pushed people forward or back, but when he got to Johnny, he lingered. He ordered him to lose the sunglasses.

"You're a little pale to be Japanese, aren't you?"

It didn't seem the kind of question that required an answer, so Johnny let it sit, and as the man took a step to go, he finally caught sight of Johnny's left cheek and stopped dead.

"Holy mother..." When the Assistant Director breathed the words on him, they smelled like grape gum being beaten to death by coffee. "Are those real?"

Johnny caught the finger before it touched his longest cork-rip of a scar.

"No," Johnny said. "I didn't feel like taking them to the cleaners today."

When he got his finger back, the Assistant Director held it to his chest like a wounded baby bird.

"Fuck it. Turn your head the other way. And remember, look at the procession, not the camera." He cut his eyes at Johnny's scars once more before raising his voice. "That goes for everybody!"

When the guy had gone, Johnny scanned the block again. His gaze ticked over a man across 1st street, a man with sunglasses on, a hat too, and a heavy tool belt. He was crew. Had to be. But he was leaning on a fake tree, staring straight at Johnny.

To take his mind off the attention, Johnny turned to the kid next to him and asked about the movie. The boy responded like he'd memorized a press release. Apparently, the production was making history with its frank portrayal of Internment. As Johnny was trying to figure out what 'frank portrayal' meant in this context, he got hit with the kid's take on Ben Silver.

Apparently, an article in the *Times* had won him over. In it, Silver called Internment a uniquely American tragedy. And, the kid added, he was Jewish, so the guy understood what camps could do to families. He whispered that last bit, nodding so solemnly at his own words that Johnny couldn't help but thank him for the information and turn away. It was perfect timing.

A bullhorn told the cattle to get ready. Nearby, the hearse engine turned over. When the water came down, it drowned everything else out. Johnny didn't have to act uneasy. His leaking umbrella, aching kidneys, and the still-staring man did it all for him.

History. The kid's h-word troubled Johnny most of all. Sure, he was Japanese-American. Maybe he was still, but it was complicated. He'd lived in Japan almost all his life. He'd served her, put on the uniform. The only ties he had to America were the language, the music and movies he loved, and his name. Nothing else was American about Johnny Ban. Yet now he moved amongst a people who seemed to speak only in ownership pronouns. *Our. Us.* But this history never felt like Johnny's. His white American father's father had flown in the Pacific and dropped firebombs on Tokyo. His Japanese mother's father had been conscripted in Hiroshima and was racing bullets in Burma when half his family ashed up and blew away in the wind. That was Johnny's history. His blood had never been fenced-in.

His was the bomber and the bombed.

NEW TOKYO HOTEL

A few minutes later, Johnny seized his chance and slipped up the block. He felt hot eyes on his back when he buzzed at the entrance to the New Tokyo Hotel, and the feeling didn't leave him when he scaled a wooden staircase that dead-ended at a wall. This place was all hallways. Where a lobby office should have been, it had a sliding window that looked in on a desk.

The girl behind the glass was pretty but her clothes didn't know it yet. A shapeless, hibiscus-print shirt held sway over her top half. With both elbows on the desk, she danced in place to a non-existent beat.

"Asada." Without taking his sunglasses off, Johnny spoke to those rippling flowers. "Kenji."

"Ah," she chirped, one blink away from being oblivious to his scars. "Welcome to Little Tokyo, Mister Asada. You're a pretty simple guy, huh?"

"Excuse me?"

She pointed at his beat-up leather satchel, and announced the obvious. "You sure didn't pack much."

"Oh." Johnny tapped his pockets. "I guess so."

"My grandmother said when a man packs too light, he carries too much baggage around inside." The hibiscus-girl studied his forehead like it might sprout flowers. "But that couldn't possibly be true of you."

Johnny smiled. "It couldn't possibly."

The girl smiled right back as he fudged a signature, and she was quick with the key. Before he took it, he told her that if anyone asked for him to send them straight to his room, then he retreated down the hallway and hid himself in the nearest doorjamb.

He waited a minute. When he was certain he had been too paranoid, the downstairs door opened and a parade of jingling and thumping came up the stairs.

A baseball-capped man presented himself at the window with that same straight-backed, military bearing. He held a pair of sunglasses in his hand, and he tucked them into his back collar like he was putting an arrow in a tiny quiver. His black, long-sleeve t-shirt read, 'Allergic 2 Snitches!!' in white capital letters, and bunched around a tool belt. It was the staring man all right. None other.

He wanted to know about the guy who just came in, and he described Johnny to the girl. He was definitely American.

Beet salad. That was what he called the scars on Johnny's face. Said he was an old friend. But then he used a name. Johnny's real name. That confused the girl, and Johnny too for that matter, but she passed his room number on like he had asked, and when the American headed up the stairs, Johnny followed.

This man moved like sharks swim. The pockets of his khaki cargo shorts hung full, low, and black vines of tattoos disappeared beneath socks bunched over combat boots.

Johnny waited until he topped the last step to rush in, to dig his pill bottle cap-first into the guy's back like it was a pistol barrel, but that back and those large white letters spun away from him, and a hand pushed hard on his spine, smashing his face into the wall, scars-first, before a ripping motion tore the bottle from his hand.

"That was rude of me, John. I'm very sorry you made me do that. I'd like an apology from you now too."

The man worked a one-handed grip on the back of Johnny's head. Still trying to differentiate wall-stains from floating spots, Johnny apologized. The pressure left his neck, and a disappointed exhale gusted over him.

"Your plate healed good," the man said.

Johnny slung a hand through his hair as he turned, cold questions beading his eyes.

"Hey, you need to turn that down. I'm not the enemy. I'm just working on-set, about to go rig this bastard-heavy light to a slider when I look over and see you in the crowd-shot. Man, talk about cosmic coincidence! I almost fell over. So I keep my eye out, and I see you come in here. I follow in anyway, to make sure, and then I get jumped with some goddamn pharmaceuticals." He took a step forward and the floor groaned sharply under his boot. He smelled like sunscreen. "It's Hector, man! Hector Ramirez. You don't remember?"

There was sadness in his voice. Real hurt. Johnny kept on staring. He kept trying to find this face in his mind and failing. This Hector had a dorsal fin nose, one that looked like it had been punched flat from both sides. He was younger than Johnny, late twenties maybe.

"It's the gourd, huh? That's cool. I mean, it's not cool, but I get it, you know?" Hector pulled his shirt up so high that a webbing of pitted scars emerged, tangled in black chest hair. It wasn't so much a healed wound as it was a cemetery dug up by blind grave robbers. "Personally, I still can't breathe sometimes. Feels like concrete..."

His sentence didn't want to finish, so he pinned a smile on it, pulled his shirt down, and changed gears.

"I'm doing a bad job ringing bells around here." Hector took a good hard look at his hands before slapping an imploring look on Johnny. "Najaf? Coalition Hospital? I never could forget a Japanese dude talking better English than me. Of course you *were* a damn translator. Your babbling kept me sane, man."

A prickling sensation worked the back of Johnny's scalp. There was something familiar about him, his voice perhaps, or the way he talked. Somehow, Johnny felt certain he had known the man. That didn't make it easier. It made it worse.

Just then, Hector's walkie-talkie spewed an acronym-laced film-speak that weighed down the corners of his mouth.

"Sorry, man. Gotta go," he said. "Lunch, okay? I'll find you."

"Sure." Johnny had no doubt he would. "Lunch."

Hector excused himself, turned, then stopped. He tossed the pill bottle back. "Don't go pulling that on anyone else." He had an easy smile, this young man. Genuine. "Good to see you, man. For real."

Then he was gone, his boots punishing the stairs, his tool belt singing all the way.

And for all this, Johnny couldn't recall a single thing about the hospital, and certainly not Hector. Not their talks. Not his face. Nothing else was more capable of making him feel like a stranger in his own body.

Inside the room, behind a locked door, Johnny took a dim view of his own intelligence, his guile. Hector had proved that trying to be smart didn't pay, and if he pulled a stunt like that on the wrong guy he would be lying on a cold shelf, tenting up a sheet with his face.

Johnny had been smart once. That was the worst part. He still remembered what it felt like to have uninterrupted thoughts, to be able to read a book without stopping and resting his eyes, to actually remember people. He had been able to think things through before the shrapnel burrowed into his face and popped out the other side.

But the bomb decided it didn't just want to wreck his skull, it wanted to change his personality. His head injury had made him impatient and impulsive.

Now, he had to try to stick people up with pill bottles. Now, he just got headaches. Now, he had to medicate—and tap his pockets. Now, everyone was a quicker thinker.

And they were younger. And their brains were still whole. If he were a computer, he would need to be recycled to make way for the newest model. A memory upgrade wasn't worth it. His processor was almost out, and his battery wasn't much better.

For the hundredth time since he saw her picture, Johnny wondered what Emi had been up to all these years, how she had

31

changed. If she ever thought of him. If she was better off than he was. She had to be.

Johnny listed his assets to the wall. A tiny, rented apartment overlooking only the most picturesque of Osaka's bus stations. A military disability pension. Two bank accounts rubbled by his ex-wife's alimony. He wasn't the first man to marry a stripper with the expectation that she'd be mildly faithful, just the stupidest.

Johnny added the three, subtracted nine from seven, carried the one, and still came up negative.

Not that the wall cared.

The sound of birds chirping came from Johnny's pocket. A whole tree full. He picked Oni's phone up, pressed a button, and said hello.

"You have arrived," Oni purred. "Good. Call any time."

The line clicked like a purse closing.

It was reasonable to assume that he was being watched, would always be watched, from here on out. Johnny thought about how to change that, thought as hard and as long as he could, thought himself onto the tingling bridge between headache and migraine, but he got nothing.

He solved the problem by going to sleep.

He shouldn't have.

ROOM 314

The phone woke him. Not Oni's phone. The one in the room. The thick plastic thing blurred its little red light in his face, screaming like a pterodactyl on the swoop.

"Hello?" Sleep had swapped Johnny's voice for a foghorn.

"You said two o'clock!" It was fast, mad Japanese.

"Did I?"

Johnny didn't recognize the caller. It was a man's voice, a livewire in his ear, complete with heavy breathing and sparks of anxiety.

"'Two o'clock. Kyoto Grand Hotel Garden. Bring the money.' That is absolutely what you said. Now the hour hand is on the two, and you are definitely not here!"

Johnny tilted the receiver away from him but kept the mouthpiece close. "Where is here?"

It came out more existential than he meant it. Johnny wanted cross-streets, an address. Instead, he got a muffled howl of disappointment.

"Kyoto Grand," the voice stopped itself. "I refuse to play your game! You know damn well where it is. You picked the meeting place!"

The line went dead. Johnny let it punish his ear for a moment before marshaling his joints to hang the thing on its cradle.

The clock on the nightstand said it was two and change. His room didn't have a toilet, so Johnny sock-footed it down the hall to the shared facilities, pissed more blood, and then hit his face with three blasts of water when two wouldn't do the trick.

His stomach reminded him he was hungry. His head told him he had dodged a migraine, but that it might be back again sometime before the end of the day. His jetlag was still there, lurking.

He ignored all of it and went back to his room to take his medicine and check the list. There was no Kyoto Grand on it. Emi hadn't been seen there.

Whatever the call was, it was for Kenji. He had been a busy little frog.

Johnny rang the front desk. A honeyed voice answered, the kind you would want to wake up to.

"Kyoto Grand Hotel," he said. "How do I get there?"

"Is everything satisfactory, sir?"

Apparently, he was good at flustering people today.

"I have a meeting there. The Garden." When that was greeted with a hanging pause, he added, "Business."

"Oh," she cooed, "oh."

He took advantage of that relief, running down the list in his hand. She gave him addresses for every last one, even though she needed a phone book for one of them—the club called The Soft Spot.

Re-suited and re-heeled, he met the owner of the voice on his way out. She was yoga-thin and muscled in all the right places. A white sweater topped her high-cut blouse like whipped cream on a chocolate pie wedge. She was in her mid-forties, but possessed an ageless beauty that every woman claws for but only five or six ever get. Her chin was firm though. She had taken some shots in her time, and as if to prove it, her hair was a glossy silver—every last light-hugging thread.

"Hello," he said, still not yet free of the foghorn. "I just called."

"Yes, Mister Asada," the silver woman replied, "how can I help?"

When he drew close, she blinked. Her light brown eyes were on the beet salad, as Hector had called it, but not uncomfortably so. She formed a question with her lips, but didn't dare speak it. She seemed happy to have an excuse to look somewhere else when he asked her to draw him a map to the Kyoto Grand, and her lines came out calligraphic on the torn notebook paper, slinking up 1st to Los Angeles Street before zipping left one block to 2nd. Johnny pocketed the directions, said thanks, and goodbye.

KYOTO GRAND

When the elevator doors opened, Johnny turned left into a two-tiered, rooftop garden the size of a grand ballroom. Ten different kinds of trees formed a green blockade along its borders. Beneath it, a restaurant with more waiters than tables perched its glass walls on the edge of a stone-bottomed pond. A wooden bridge separated this pool from its source, a waterfall with granite buckteeth grinning through its cascade.

Johnny didn't see anybody, so he took the bridge and climbed stairs to the garden's top level. The sunny afternoon smelled of jasmine, and speakers stuck to decorative lampposts spat out music that ruined the feel of the place. Johnny could deal with ugly waterfalls, but Muzaked jazz made him want to take a flying leap.

His likely caller, a man in a rumpled suit, stood at the roof's edge, looking out at a white, chess bishop of a chapel tower across the street. Flagpoles riveted to the hotel ledge extended past trees, framing the man on either side: Japan's rising sun, and the Stars and Stripes. Johnny couldn't help feeling that the man purposely placed himself between them.

To the wrinkled gray pinstripes, he said, "Somebody else must have called you."

The man turned. He had a sweaty-pale face, hollow cheeks. He had probably been awake for two solid days.

"I could only get two hundred thousand," the man said.

"Listen, someone else called you. I think I know who did, but—"

The man ripped his sunglasses off, revealing wide, begging eyes.

"Please understand. One million is too much!" He loosened his tie before whispering the rest. "Take it. Please?"

He shoved a small leather bag at Johnny. It had a belt wrapped around it, and the buckle hit him in the gut.

Johnny didn't move. Didn't take it. He knew this man. His stomach knew first. It did a barrel roll and dived for his shoes.

"Mister Sato," he blurted.

Emi Sato's father rolled back on his heels like he had been struck. Whatever reserve he had left popped.

"Please, tell me where Emi is! You have tortured us long enough!" Mr. Sato lurched and teetered, hugging the duffel like it was alive, like it was a swaddled baby girl.

"Calm down, sir. As far as I know, no kidnapping took place."

"You told me you had her!"

"I did not call, sir." Johnny couldn't tell the whole story, so he skipped a few things. "I knew your daughters when we were kids. I happen to be looking for Emi now, and I will find her. Somehow. I promise."

A debt unpaid. That was what a promise was. Johnny knew it. He didn't take it lightly. Couldn't. His stomach wouldn't let him.

It was clear that since Kenji knew Emi's real name, he had been playing both sides, and maybe masqueraded as a kidnapper to a girl he didn't know the whereabouts of yet. Maybe it was under Oni's orders.

It was a bold play, a play that depended an awful lot on the girl never contacting her parents, but if Mr. Sato's hysterics were anything to go by, they had gambled rightly. Then again, they might know they gambled right. Emi Sato might be dead somewhere, but if that were the case, they wouldn't have bothered to send Johnny.

"How can I believe you?" Mr. Sato sagged, stared at his shoes. This was progress. "Why were you at the number they gave me?"

"Bad luck," Johnny said. It wouldn't do the man any good to know he had been set up too. "Now, Mister Sato, I need to know why you never reported Emi missing all those years ago. How long has she been gone?"

Redness rushed over Mr. Sato's throat and ears. The man looked like he was going to explode if he didn't speak, and when he opened his mouth, anguish snatched at his eyes.

"It was my fault! You could never understand! She hated school. The bullies. She hated it more than she wanted to live. Emi was going to... going to kill herself. She tried twice." Mr. Sato's pupils churned themselves into black, grasping things. Looking into them was like looking down the throats of famished baby birds. "I had to do something, so I sent her away. To my associate in Osaka. She was good with numbers. She could work the books. Could learn to. But he neglected to teach her. Instead, he made her what she is. Made her a monster."

Johnny felt his heartbeat in his ears. "What do you mean a monster?"

Mr. Sato's whole body snapped at Johnny, stopped six good centimeters from touching. He could smell the man. The slept-in clothes. The gin-sweat and the panic.

"I need her back! You understand?" Mr. Sato's mouth hung open, and inside, the tongue worked back-and-forth as his forehead crumbled into wrinkles. "I have to *atone*."

Johnny had no reply, only a hot feeling on his neck that wouldn't go away. He took a step backward. Took two.

Mr. Sato sagged where he was standing. The man blinked twice before his gaze wandered up to the sky. He was finally losing the thread.

"How did you get your scars?"

"I fought a panther once," Johnny said, his skull buzzing beneath his scalp. "I won."

Mr. Sato's eyes turned inward. "It must have been terrible."

Johnny nodded. "Where are you staying?"

Mr. Sato pointed at the tower busy casting its shadow on the garden. Room 707, he said. A palindrome. Unforgettable, he said.

Johnny wrote it down anyway. He was the only person he knew who could forget those kinds of things.

"Get some rest, sir. I will call when I know something."

Johnny took the next elevator and padded a fast beat over the red lobby carpet studded with black flower patterns, grappling with the information that Emi hadn't run away at all. That she had never even been missing in the first place. She had been sent away. Made a *monster* somehow. And if she was made into one, there had to be a purpose.

Off the top of his damaged head, Johnny could only come up with one. Prostitution. He couldn't think of anything more monstrous to a father than that.

The acid in his stomach kicked up at the thought. His lungs didn't appreciate it. They would have gotten a bath if Johnny hadn't dismissed the idea the second he pictured Emi disrobing, covered in her pink continents. Most men would never think her beautiful. Not in Japan. A hooker like that could never make enough to survive. Emi Sato had to be some other kind of monster.

And Johnny had to find out, had to know what could possibly make a father act like that, because he couldn't shake Mr. Sato's expression. It was the kind that said he had one thing left to live for, and he didn't know if he would ever see it again. That look had crawled under Johnny's skin and kicked around in his ribs.

But it couldn't be helped. He had been stupidly sensitive to faces ever since he lost part of his.

Johnny tapped his pockets, grabbed the list out, and ran it down: Karaoke Weekend, Nishi Temple, and The Soft Spot. He decided he might as well hit the first one, and asked the valet for directions to 3rd and Alameda.

He hadn't even stepped onto the sidewalk when a plummeting form beat him there. He thought it was a swooping raven at first.

It wasn't. Ravens didn't wear gray suits.

Mr. Sato hit the street with a fast-fluttering smack that sounded like a two-by-four punching into a watermelon.

He landed with his suit coat covering his face. In and out gasps dented gray pinstripes like fish gills flapping open, flapping shut.

Beside Johnny, someone screamed. But he didn't turn to the noise. He looked up.

A quick head, covered with a low baseball cap and sunglasses, ducked back into the garden, out of view.

Tearing the jacket from Mr. Sato's face, Johnny ripped a sleeve off and bolted it into a tourniquet. The man's legs were stuck in a synchronized swimming position. Except they each faced a different direction. Half a shinbone had decided to take a holiday outside his skin.

As Johnny tied the sleeve off above it, the wound puckered and spat like a child's mouth trying to make like a motorboat. He didn't notice the blood seeping from Mr. Sato's skull until after the sirens wailed into earshot.

DOWNTOWN

"Please describe the person you saw immediately after this Sato fell to his death." Detective Rooney sat at his keyboard, ready to take Johnny's statement.

A lower house Diet member gone AWOL had the bad sense to die a block from L.A.P.D. headquarters, two blocks from the *Times*, and within minutes everyone on earth knew it. The Japanese media appeared out of thin air, camped out around the water sculpture outside, and wouldn't leave until they got a statement.

"Dark baseball cap with a light logo," Johnny replied. "White or yellow. Black sunglasses with black lenses. Dark turtleneck pulled up over the jaw. That's it."

Pale-blue-shirted, navy-blue-tied, and with his pepper hair turning to salt just above his ears, Detective Gerald Rooney's eyes were set too closely together, right on the borders of his nose.

The squad room bullpen was stuck between shifts. Of the twenty-two gunmetal desks, only three were occupied. Johnny sat in a black chair next to one of them, the sidecar to Rooney's motorcycle.

"In your opinion," Rooney said, "man or woman?"

"Man, I think." Johnny shifted in his chair. "He was three stories up, sir. He moved like a scared rabbit, so I thought he pushed Mister Sato."

Johnny conveniently left out the part about knowing the victim, much less having spoken to him moments before his death. If he had, Rooney might have listened more closely. As it was, he didn't seem to care. The detective closed his notepad and leaned forward.

"Mister Asada, I'd like you to do us a favor and not mention this to anyone." When Rooney said anyone, he meant the reporters outside. "We'll follow it up."

Johnny nodded. He knew what that meant. Mr. Sato would likely be classified as a suicide, and it was for the best. Rooney didn't need to know there was a missing bag with two hundred grand in it.

"Nice skin art," he said, nodding at Johnny's scars. They were purple-brown under the fluorescent lights, like a child's hand had thumb-painted four random craters down his cheek. "Shrapnel?"

Johnny shrugged. "Microwave accident."

"Like hell. Where'd you grow them?"

"Samawah," Johnny said. When he could see it didn't ring any bells for the detective, he added, "Iraq."

"Goddamn." Rooney whistled. "Didn't even know they sent Japanese boys over there. Learn something new everyday. What brings you to my city, Mister Asada?"

My. Johnny sniffed at the pronoun. It seemed to him that everyone owned everything in America, even things that weren't theirs alone.

Johnny smiled a little and looked down at his hands. He could lie or level. He chose the latter.

"I'm looking for someone," he said.

"What kind of someone?"

"Ex-girlfriend. Disappeared years ago. I was told she was in L.A. Her family would like to know she's safe."

It was true enough, but Johnny had left out the if — *if* she was safe. That wasn't guaranteed yet.

"You working for the family?"

"No."

Mr. Sato's look, the one that didn't know if it could go on, bumped around under Johnny's skin. It shot goosebumps down the back of his neck. He would be seeing those eyes again whenever he closed his.

"What does she look like?"

"Five foot seven, one hundred and fifteen pounds. Black hair. Thin nose. Full lips. Brown eyes." Johnny thought about her ears, her chin, how pigmented islands floated on that pale sea, and then he made the conscious decision to lie. "Fair skin."

The moment it left his lips, Johnny knew he was all in. It didn't matter what Oni wanted her for. Johnny needed to see Emi for himself.

Rooney grunted. "There's only about two million Asian women in this county that fit that description."

"Maybe you can put an A.P.B. out."

"I'll get right on that." Rooney smiled. It was a tired twitch, one that drooped at the edges and might have turned frown at any moment, but it did the job. It masked his unease.

Only creepy-love cases flew halfway around the world for old girlfriends like that. Rooney gestured to the door to let the man know he was free to go.

Rooney had already been on fourteen hours today. Two more than his shift, thanks to the 2nd Street Skydiver. Two more he wouldn't get paid for, thanks to the new city restrictions on overtime.

Johnny bowed. He exited by the same glass doors he came in through. He would be seeing Rooney and his coffee-stained cuffs again. Sure, he would.

And it wouldn't go so smoothly next time either.

GRAND AGAIN

With the day hanging on his neck like a hot cotton towel, Johnny pounded sidewalk down 2nd, back to the Kyoto Grand.

There weren't any cops in the garden. Johnny gave it a quick once-over, as good as he could without tipping off the hotel security. The bag wasn't behind any perimeter trees. Wasn't stashed in a bush or under a table. Wasn't in either lip of the terraced levels below the flags, not in the drainage area, and not in the six-foot width of tiled walkway built for the silver mouths of air conditioning exhaust pipes.

By the time Johnny got back to East 1st Street, his will to keep going had faded. But 1st Street was doing the opposite just to spite him: the circus had finally put up its tent.

Poled up behind sawhorse barriers that told cars to go around, the makeshift wardrobe tent had been moved to the middle of the street and inside it, fifty voices were raised to war whoops.

Johnny looped around this carnival, but his jetlag was an impressionable thing. Once it heard three Panzer-size generators rumbling together in Koyasan Temple's arterial driveway, it started rumbling too. A sympathy rumble, inside his head. Only sleep cured that one, and it would have, if a damp-limp hand hadn't grabbed his elbow.

The wet fingers belonged to a kid with a haircut like a mushroom top.

"Found him," the mouth beneath the hair-cap spat into a microphone cord dangling from an ear. "I found Scarface!"

Johnny was thinking how getting a nickname meant he was coming up in the world when a familiarly big-bellied man pushed through a crowd of excited women trying on hats. The Assistant Director glared at the kid straight off.

"Thank you, *Jesse*," the guy hissed. He wiped his sweaty face with a sheet of paper, threw it to the ground.

The kid scuttled away, but not before one last look at Johnny's beet salad.

"Listen, big news for you, my friend, the good kind. What's your name anyway?"

Through the dull rumble, Johnny still had the presence of mind to say, "Kenji."

"Awesome," he said. "Perfect. My name's Barry, by the way. Plain Barry, like the fruit, except with an A."

Barry tried a grin. It failed. He transitioned to the most serious face he could muster, but before it set, a voice buzzed loud in his headset, and he blinked like a cat being strapped into a party hat: all big-eyed annoyance and quaking chin. He shook it off.

"So, anyway, Ben Silver, right? The director? He *loves* your face. Thinks it's really real. Let's walk and talk." Barry guided him right back where he had started, the front of the barking carnival tent. "So we need you more, okay? Just a few shots. Is that a problem?"

It was the appropriate time for Johnny to tell the man to go to hell, but his mind was elsewhere, stuck on how doughy Mr. Sato's twisted legs felt in his hands, like they didn't have any bones in them at all. Before he knew it, he was passed off to a freckled flamingo of a girl—one with the blondest of blonde hair—as Barry ran his eyes over Johnny's shirt and whispered haltingly into his headset.

"Make-up, are you putting blood on people?"

SHABU-SHABU HOUSE

Filled with the clinking of sauce bowls, the restaurant was a great big shoebox of a room with a glass front lipped in cement. A semi-circular counter extended to the back wall like half a race-track with a wide center aisle that workers sped up and down. Customers sat on the outside, leaning over individual hot pots. Up front, a man in chef whites cut red meat thin as rice paper on a butcher slicer.

At the counter, Hector gave Johnny the slow eye.

"You're not so good at saying no, are you, John? Why get roped into the movie?"

Johnny had gone back for his shoes after he left the set because he had walked off in the costume-sandals. When he got to his hotel room and found the door slightly ajar, he took no chances. He went downstairs, asked for his bag to be moved to one that overlooked 1st Street, and slid a hundred-dollar bill over the desk. The hibiscus-girl joked it would take hours to move all his luggage, but she obliged.

He ran into Hector outside the hotel right after, and that promised lunch ended up an early dinner.

"Don't you have anything better to do?" Hector eyed him like he was due an explanation.

Johnny couldn't explain that it was a whole host of reasons smashing together in his head. The shock, maybe. Mr. Sato, definitely. The jetlag, sure. But Johnny couldn't explain the smaller causes to Hector either, like how good it felt for someone to like his face, for any reason. So he didn't.

He didn't spill about the Super Harmony Theatre either, how Mr. Leonard Ellis had taken him there for English lessons when he was barely a teenager. *Real world language application*, the man had said. Back then, the Harmony only ran classics. The kind of black and white movies where the leads talked too fast, and kissed even faster. That dialogue made Johnny's head spin, never more so than when he got quizzed on plots and slang.

But there was something more there too. Through those flickering examples, Ellis showed him how a man was only as big as what made him angry, that the best kind of man was often defined by what he didn't do, or what he didn't say, and in that theater, teenage Johnny pictured himself up there on the screen every Wednesday matinee. In his naivety, he used to think that if he were strong enough or good enough Emi Sato might come back, that she might breeze in out of nowhere and surprise him, like the blondes in all those films.

Johnny put his chopsticks down and lowered his voice. It was as good a time as any to have it out.

"Hector," he said, "I don't remember you from the desert."

"So kick loose, right? Fill in your lost days?"

"If you can manage it."

"Not sure I can, John. I was in and out myself." Hector tapped his chest like Johnny tapped pockets, like he was trying to remember what he put there. "I know some. Like, how you got your name from your sailor daddy, Johnny after Johnny Cash, and then your mama dragged you back to Japan after trying for, like, nine years to reconcile with your pops, and you got to the land where everybody was the same, and it was like you might as well have been named Sue." Hector let off a sad, slow laugh. "Gotta be the worst place in the world to grow up different, man. But just like that song, it made you tough, right? Fists got keen and your wits got hard."

Johnny didn't give any indication that Hector was right about him, or that he had gotten the lyric wrong. Keenness was for wits, hardness for fists.

"Why's this feel like a test, John?"

"Because it is."

Hector sighed and speared a half-leaf of cabbage floating on the rolling boil in front of him. He was good with chopsticks, like he had been using them for years. Johnny was surprised to see how similar their hands were: thick, knotted cigars of fingers with bulges at the joints. Boxer's hands. In Japan, their size had always marked Johnny as different, as less than pure, and now that he finally fit in somewhere he didn't know how to feel about it.

"I know you married a Japanese-Israeli girl," Hector said, "probably the only one on earth. She was half like you. The Japanese Jewess, you called her. But you talked more about Emi. You'd babble about maps and scars with her, man. Yin-Yang Girl, you said. Yogurt Face. Her grill was messed up, right?"

Satisfied that this man did indeed know him, Johnny picked his chopsticks up and extricated a wrinkled little ball of beef from the boil. He slid Emi's picture to Hector under the counter.

"*Man*." In Hector's world, the word was a Swiss Army knife. It had multiple uses, and all depended on intonation. This one drew itself out in awe. "Those cheekbones could cut glass. Is she here? Maybe?"

Johnny brought Hector almost up to speed. He said he hurt Kenji, hurt him bad, but left out the ending. He told Hector about Oni, about the flight. The eight days. Mr. Sato's base jump. Detective Rooney. His hotel room door being open. His moving. And how Emi might be dead.

Hector took it all in. When he finally decided to talk, his response surprised Johnny in its earnestness.

"Let me *in*, John. Four hands are better than two. In a way, you saved my life back there. I would've gone crazy in that hospital if it wasn't for you, brother." Hector hit him with a stone-serious gaze that knew IEDs too, had felt one. It was an honor-heavy thing between them. A bond from being wounded, from bleeding, and from being put back together on an operating table only to heal raggedly in adjacent beds. "And now I got the itch. I got your disease. Everybody that ever got close to bedsores has it. That Say-Yes-To-Everything Virus. My therapist says I'm an adrenaline head now. Thrill-junkie, she says. And you know what? She's right."

Johnny knew he couldn't refuse. Not then.

"There are some bad folks involved," he said. "It's all bad news."

"That's just the kind I like writing."

Johnny smiled. His beet salad crinkled up on his cheek. "When did you get out?"

"Last year." Hector's eyes prowled the silver troughs hanging upside down from the ceiling to vent steam. "They pressed me for a re-up. I wasn't having it. War isn't war anymore, John. You know that. It's private. It's contracted out now, government-bidded."

For a moment, Johnny was taken back to Iraq. He thought about wiring right then, about late orders and uncontrollable Samawah supply chains.

"Man, my pops fought in Nam. You think he had to put up with bullets so private security firms could run around and cash checks? I mean, I got thirty a year plus room, terrible board, and an iffy G.I. Bill?" He counted those out on his fingers, one, two, three. "But these dudes are making six figures for two months and sporting the best gear on earth? Who's guarding these people with no rules? The uniforms are. Who's enforcing the peace zone so mercenaries can roll around and head-shot civilians? Me and you and every other unlucky enlisted."

Red exasperation ribboned on his cheeks, and then it slipped away. His voice came back quiet. "Murder isn't murder to them, John. It's *marketing*. *It's brand management*."

Johnny shivered a tight, cold shiver that slipped down his spine and ended up in his ankles.

"So of course a firm had to go and contact me when I got out. Heard I was recommended, they said."

The waitress came by to turn off their burners. She asked if they needed anything else. They both shook their heads in unison.

When she was gone Johnny asked Hector if he took the job.

"Man." The word accessorized itself with a scoff, a smile, and a backward nod before Hector shook his tool belt. "What do *you* think?"

LITTLE TOKYO MARKETPLACE

Inside the slab of concrete masquerading as a mall on 3rd and Alameda, Johnny and Hector knew the second they walked in that they had found the land that dollars forgot.

Not a single shop was open on the left-hand side, only a straight row of floor-to-ceiling glass covered in butcher paper from the inside. Across from it, two dessert places sat locked in a shoulder-to-shoulder grudge match. Cream puffs had the edge on frozen yogurt, two customers to none.

In the middle of it all sat an escalator bank. Only up worked. A backlit directory missing half the store names sat nearby. Sweat-yellow light shone through those empty, rectangular holes like a razor-bladed lampshade. Johnny scanned it anyway. When he hopped the escalator, Hector followed.

Three stores on the second floor had their metal gates closed. Plastic chairs molded to look like rocks made a sad little Zen garden in the middle of a scuffed tile sea.

Johnny marked the entrance to the karaoke place at first glance, but he was momentarily more interested in sightlines. He took two steps, looking for the best angle and found it in one: Muramasa Swords and Novelties sat diagonally across from his target of interest, and that meant it had a perfect vantage point.

Everything about the man at the counter screamed Rice King. Caucasian, bespectacled, bald as a tortoise, and connoisseur of all things Japanese, the man wore a costume kimono and broke up the expanse between his eyebrows and his gleaming head with a rising sun bandanna.

"How's business?" Johnny eyed the front display case. Its three shelves were packed with knives of all sizes, some good, some no better than toys.

"What happened to your face?" The Rice King smiled childishly.

Johnny sniffed and thumbed his nose. Two small speakers droned talk radio from a shelf behind the man. The body of the slain American businessman, Edward Galt, was being shipped home from Osaka. Police were actively searching for the gunman and his accomplice, a getaway driver. Three soldiers had been killed in a convoy ambush in Afghanistan.

Hector winced at that.

"You don't have to tell me," the Rice King said. "Do you speak Japanese?"

"Only when I run out of English."

"That's great you can speak it!" The man couldn't hide his enthusiasm. What was more, he seemed to mean it.

Johnny blinked. For a fat second he fought back the feeling that if his father had been more like this man, he might have stuck around. His last name might have stayed Wells instead of changing, in defeat, to his mother's Ban.

"What do you know about," the man leaned in, and his voice tumbled down to confidentiality, "the Meiji Era?"

Hector laughed. The man narrowed his eyes at him before swinging his chin back to Johnny.

"I'm writing a book! It's got mythology and swordplay and historical parts! It's about honor and blood. Want to read it? I have copies."

Seven hundred and forty printed pages slapped the counter so hard the glass creaked.

Johnny held up Emi's picture. "Have you seen her?"

"Wow-oh-wow," he shouted. "She's so beautiful!"

"Is that a no?" Johnny was getting tired of the act.

The Rice King cocked his head. "We have the finest knives ever made. Knives that saved kingdoms!"

Johnny caught the hint. It was about as subtle as smelling salts.

"You want one?" He eyed Hector. "I'm buying."

Inside of four seconds, Ramirez stubbed a finger at a pearl-handled, stiletto switchblade.

"Always wanted one of them," he said.

"An excellent choice! Really it's—"

Ben Franklin cut the Rice King off.

"The knuckles too," Johnny said. He pointed at a matching set of steel ones. He laid out three more green kite-flyers on the table next to the first and made a set of wigged quadruplets—two more than any of it was worth. "Have you seen the girl now?"

"I have." The man turned, disappeared into the back store-room, and came back carrying the ugliest sword Johnny had ever seen. "This is the blade Musashi Miyamoto used!"

Johnny looked at Hector, who bullied the counter with a lean. His tool belt punched at the glass, and the surface groaned like it was going to give way.

"Uh, I saw her go into the karaoke. I love *enka!*"

The Rice King belted out six sad notes and six bad pronunciations in as many syllables. It might have been *Uwasa no Onna* if the ballad ever deserved such torture.

"Just say when," Hector told Johnny.

If the Rice King had fallen in a manhole his singing couldn't have stopped faster.

"Twice." The man's larynx did a double dip, and after that his voice came out as a Midwestern drone rasping over soft syllables. "Didn't leave though. She, uh, must've gone after I closed."

"Did you see her with anyone?"

The answer came too fast. "No."

"A guy or a girl?"

His headband graying with sweat-dots, the Rice King's gaze sprinted to the broken down escalator.

His body wasn't going with it.

"You know I still got meat in my teeth?" Hector flicked the switch open. He slid its blade between a lower incisor and its flat neighbor.

"She didn't go *in* with anyone, but a man in a suit met her out, uh, out front both times."

"Who is he?"

"Kawari." His eyes were big as baseballs. "Keizo Kawari. Don't tell him I said. *Please.* He'll kill me."

Johnny wheeled away. Hector was right beside him, folding his blade back into its housing and laughing like sandpaper dancing over metal.

"Living your whole life wanting to be something you're not and never could be, *man.*" He snorted. "What's that like?"

Johnny knew, but he wouldn't say it felt like being an ostrich, standing with his feet planted firmly on a plain, and sure, he looked up at birds in flight, but he knew he'd never get off the ground like they did.

So Johnny Ban just tapped his pockets, slipped cold steel over his knuckles, pulled his sleeves down as far as they would go, and wondered how much longer he could make it without sleep.

KARAOKE WEEKEND

A cursive whip of neon buzzed pinkly inside the entrance of the first place on Johnny's list, shining its light on a pair of forked hallways just beyond an oblong front desk. A squirrel-faced boy sitting there was trying his hardest to read manga. He looked dumber than a bucket of paste, so Johnny hit him with a quick burst of Japanese to unsettle him.

"The man in the suit," he said, "where is he?"

"What suit?" The boy ruffled his jet-black hair in the most practiced manner possible.

"Kawari. Where is he?"

The boy blinked like the simple process of listening was painful.

"Thanks for nothing," Johnny replied, already moving down the near hallway and peering in windows.

"Hey," the boy said to his back, "you forgot to pay!"

Hector shot the kid a sit-down look and took the far hallway. The whole place was a catacomb, one packed with tiny singing rooms instead of tombs. Each studio had bare gray walls. Each was stocked with bad leather sinkholes pretending to be couches, and big old televisions spilling half-light over singers closing their eyes on the high notes. The whole place sounded like parrots fighting.

Hector raised his voice. "You know what, John? Sometimes it's okay to judge a book by its cover. You wouldn't want to read everything. You couldn't."

Johnny smiled and said, "Found him."

This room was different. It had two deep red walls and one white one, recessed lighting, a black couch pinned into the back corner with a coffee table longer than a bowling alley in front of it, and a ceiling-mounted television projector that didn't even bother with a screen, it just shot its images onto the near white wall.

Keizo Kawari had one foot up on the coffee table and was throat-deep in a ballad when Johnny kicked the door in.

It was *Tsubasa wo Kudasai* and it wasn't half-bad. He was a cool customer, this Keizo. The interruption hadn't even creased his face. That was fine by Johnny. Everybody was tough until the first shot. Johnny squeezed the sweat-hot metal of steel knuckles in both palms. Everybody was tough until they couldn't breathe.

Hector pushed into the room. "You know, it's rude putting your foot up like that. Other people use this room too. Show some common courtesy."

Keizo stopped singing and turned his pudding-brown eyes on them. Tinkling synths kept coming. He didn't put his foot down. Hector didn't like that.

"Man, people like you walk around breathing like nobody else has to." Hector kicked the table out from under Keizo, pitching the man forward before he caught himself. "You're welcome."

Keizo put on his best glare. Hector smirked. It didn't do anything for Johnny either. It was low-wattage stuff. Real hard rocks didn't glare.

Oni hadn't. All he had ever done was smile.

"What's this book cover tell you?" Johnny wanted to know.

"Not sure yet," Hector said as he pulled the blinds and locked the door. "Maybe take off the dust jacket?"

"Take your jacket off," Johnny translated.

Keizo shrugged his blue blazer onto the couch. He was late-forties, shorter than Johnny by half a foot and lumpy in the neck and belly.

"Looks flimsy," Hector decided. "You could read all you need in one sitting."

Keizo glanced from Johnny to Hector and back. Johnny knew the man had diagnosed his ethnicity on sight, had decided he wasn't really Japanese, and he saw superiority welling up in that face. So, it was unsurprising when Keizo addressed him in heavily accented English.

"How may I assist you?" Keizo Kawari had a speaking voice like a TV weatherman.

Johnny couldn't imagine Emi spending any time with this man. Ever. He slapped her picture to Keizo's chest, and answered in Japanese. "Where is she?"

One look at that face and Keizo's glare fell off a cliff. Tired-crinkled eyes replaced it. His mouth puckered like he had swallowed a snail just as the song trailed off.

Hector laughed and snatched a songbook off the table.

"I have no idea," Keizo replied in Japanese this time.

Maybe it was a lie, maybe it wasn't. Neither mattered.

Johnny grabbed Keizo's microphone and brained him with it. A bass thump leapt from the speakers.

"Try again." Johnny made a fist around the mic.

Keizo ran a finger over his forehead, stared at the hot blood that came back on a fingertip.

Before he could make a plea, Johnny played a two-note combination on his ribs, steel knuckles jarring so fiercely against his own that he thought he might break a few. The speakers boom-boomed.

That was when Johnny Cash came on.

The thumping rhythm guitar sounded like a rolling train. Words bigger than Johnny's head scrolled over Hector and onto the wall.

"Yeah, man!" Hector grinned. "*Yeah.*"

"Your girl is not worth finding." Keizo cradled his ribs. "If you find her, you might wish you never had."

"Who said she was my girl?"

Johnny feinted a left to the liver, and when Keizo flinched inside to block, the man's kidney caught a right hook that could've felled a calf.

Keizo dropped like a rock, split his chin on the table on the way down, and smacked floor moaning a wet moan Johnny knew all too well.

"My tears I have been a-crying for you, woman, are gonna flood that big, big river," Hector crooned, "but I'm a-gonna sit right down before I *die*!"

Some people were incapable of singing lyrics correctly even when the words were scrolling right in front of their faces. They never could and never would, and worse yet, they never knew it and never cared. Hector Ramirez was one of those people.

All the same, Johnny pounded the beat out on Keizo's stomach and the speakers broadcast every blow. When Johnny finally let up, Keizo wheezed like he had a hole in him.

"The Soft Spot," he coughed the words. "They know where she is."

"Drop a name."

Before Keizo was done shaking his wide-eyed, bloody face back and forth, Johnny ripped a cushion from the couch, put his knee into it, and leaned all his weight down on Keizo's head. The man thrashed like a caught marlin taking line, flipping the table with a wayward kick. Johnny pushed until something snapped. Then he let up.

The second the cushion left Keizo, he coughed a thick red mist three feet in the air. It rained down on songbooks and shoes, stippled Johnny's cheeks and nose.

"*Gin*," he sputtered. "*Kin*."

Johnny motioned for Hector. They hoisted Keizo onto the couch and turned him on his side so he wouldn't drown in his own blood, and it was coming fast and cherry-dark in the spinning light, pooling like syrup on the hardwood. After Hector righted the coffee table, Johnny threw a stack of Franklins on it.

"Better use that to get your shine back," Hector said. "You're looking a little dull right now, big man."

LEONARD ELLIS

The first time Johnny met Mister Ellis, the man was sitting on the stoop of his Osaka-cho apartment building, polishing his shoes.

He was a square man in every sense of the word. He had a square face and a square jaw and square-solid shoulders, and even the shoe turning itself into a black mirror beneath his buffing was square-toed. The man didn't drink. Didn't approve of drugs. Didn't listen to music that wasn't classical.

Yes, indeed, no man on earth was more responsible for Johnny being Johnny than Leonard Ellis, Chief Petty Officer, U.S. Navy, Retired.

"You're late," his new English teacher said without looking up. His close-shaven gray hair was squared off on the back of his neck. "Is this the first impression you most wish to convey?"

With a welt the size of a grape tomato gleaming under his left eye, thirteen-year-old Johnny burst into tears. Sure, one of the boys at school had smacked him, but that wasn't why he turned on the faucet.

His mother had spent years searching for a decent tutor for him, a native speaker, and Mr. Ellis was the best there was, only just retired from teaching in a Naniwa-cho language school. If she found out that it was Johnny's fault that Mr. Ellis didn't take him on, that woman would never forgive him.

Leonard Ellis took one look at the swelling on the boy's face and responded like the cruiserweight he was, and the super middleweight he had once been.

"I had some food set out upstairs, but it looks like you have been busy eating right-hooks instead." Cool brown eyes ticked over Johnny, weighed him up. Before too long he sighed and said, "Shall we go?"

The building didn't look like much on the outside. It was a corrugated thing with rust streaks at its angles like a crushed cake box leaking frosting. Johnny never would have guessed what lay behind that door, or why they had to take the train to get to it.

When Mr. Ellis tugged it open, sodden heat hit Johnny like a truck and he had to steady himself on the desk inside the entrance. Behind it, three rectangular light strips hung low on precarious ceiling cords, shining all their light on a boxing ring that sat smack in the middle of a concrete floor. Someone had painted it green. Badly.

The wooden walls were gangrenous at their shins from all the flakes that had been kicked up and re-deposited over the years. But no one in there cared.

Fighters worked the ring's edges. Some shadowboxed. Some did pushups on their fists. Some used the heavy bags on the far wall, and some jiggled lockers on the near one. Of all the places in the world, the Yamada Gym in Ebisu-cho played host to Johnny Ban's first English lesson since he had left the United States for good.

Mr. Ellis reached behind the desk and squeezed three different pairs of gloves before settling on one.

"Take these."

They made a soft hissing sound when he pushed them into Johnny's chest. Their leather was both shiny and sticky at the same time.

People here knew Leonard Ellis. He helped out with the older fighters when a fight came up. Cut-man. Corner-man. Whatever was needed. So when he waltzed in with a new kid and set up shop under the speed bags, nobody batted an eyelid, not even the owner, who was too busy yelling at three boys jumping rope.

As soon as Mr. Ellis knew Johnny was right-handed, he had the kid create a base by staggering his feet. Left foot forward, right foot back. Then he crammed Johnny's hands into gloves and put red punchpads on his own. He held them up to Johnny. They looked like fat foam circles with black target spots in their middles.

"Breathing," Mr. Ellis said, "is more important than hitting. You get your breathing right and you can outlast anybody." He set his feet. "Now I want you to make a tight fist and punch slowly on the exhale, the out-breath."

He showed Johnny three times, and then he let him try.

"Inhale when the arm comes back," he said. "Good. Take it even slower than that. Feel your weight. Put your hip into it. Turn in and flex. Good."

Mr. Ellis alternated hands, and let Johnny punch for a bit. He let the left jab/straight right combination go *thup-thup* into his mitts for a minute as he watched the boy's eyes. Watched the thinking process behind them, from the weight shift to the breathing. Johnny was a fast learner. There was no disguising it.

"You know your alphabet?" When Mr. Ellis saw Johnny nod, he said, "Hit it out. Twenty-six punches. Let's go."

Johnny did. Before he got to the letter D, Ellis could tell the boy was coordinated. He had a natural right hand. From the way he threw it to the way he landed it, there was no wasted movement.

MURAMASA SWORDS AND NOVELTIES

Johnny was halfway across the sad little rock garden, almost to the stalled down-escalator, when Hector spoke up.

"You got an aptitude for doing bad things to bad people, John. You looked like a damn boxer in there."

Johnny fought the steel off his hands and into his coat pockets. His swollen knuckles burned all in a row. He flexed them. Held them out for inspection.

Dented crescents of bluebells already marked his indexes, his middles. They promised bouquets by morning.

He had hit Keizo hard enough all right—pounded the man like he was telegraph wire, and if she was alive, Emi Sato would certainly hear those reverberations, would know he had come for her. Hopefully.

"What's 'Keen' and 'Gheen' mean anyway," Hector asked. "Are they people?"

"Gold and Silver," Johnny answered, but before he could explain further, Hector's hand fell hard across his chest.

"Something tells me we don't have eight days anymore, man."

Hector tilted his nose at Muramasa Swords and Novelties. Its lights were still on. The security gate was only a third of the way down and doing a slow trapeze-sway from its dangling place in the ceiling. Beneath it, the glass weapons case had been smashed, but not robbery-style. This was a different matter altogether.

A personal one.

The top sported a crater the size of a dinner plate, one that had obviously accommodated a grown man's forehead at a decent rate of speed, decent enough to split a skull anyway, because blood puddled in that crushed pit like a clogged sink and spread from there, globbing over edges, dragging red trails down see-through sides.

Everywhere Johnny looked, he saw signs of a struggle: a bloody handprint here, a ripped-out phone cord there, an arching shoeprint where someone had slipped in blood and fallen.

"Now I know he said someone would kill him if he said anything, but *damn*." Hector laughed. "I guess he shouldn't've told us!"

"No witnesses? No cops yet?"

Johnny slung a glance at the purse store. It was closed and gated. Ditto for two t-shirt boutiques. No one entered or exited Karaoke Weekend, and the nearby arcade spewed sounds of rapid-fire gunshots and squealing tires.

"Time to jump off then," Hector said. "We're a step ahead of the guillotine as it is, man."

Outside, a dark fog had settled in on the night, and a soggy breeze hadn't done much but hug its edges. Thick yellow circles of lamplight studded the sidewalk at thirty-foot intervals, only visible three-deep in both directions.

There were no cars at the mall meters. 3rd Street was as dead as could be.

"I hope that cat gets reborn Japanese. That'd make him happy." Hector looked at his pager, tsked at it, and put it back on his belt. "Night shoot setup. Back on duty. You good to get back?"

Before Johnny could nod, Hector clutched his tool belt and headed toward Central at a half-jog, already jingling up the night.

IRAQ

On the day an improvised explosive device tore his life apart, First Sergeant Johnny Ban had already soaked his uniform with sweat by 8:14 a.m. This was irritatingly normal, but Johnny never did get used to it. In fact, it led him to believe that the Middle East had a different sun than Japan—one capable of baking him twice, first from above, and then again as it reflected off the sand-choked Samawah streets.

On either side of that particular avenue, two rows of three-story buildings looked like crushed paper bags facing each other. A dented van and a white hatchback were parked up the block in the valley between.

Each had been checked by their British escort.

The hatchback wasn't drivable. It sat ten yards from them on three tires and a stone block, next to a shop that sold cloth from wooden sidewalk racks. Bolts fluttered under the rippling hands of children before they were chased away by an old woman's broom.

The kids rushed straight to a thin brown thing that barked like a dog, and moved like a dog, but was so thin that it seemed more like a sketch of an animal than a real one. Thinner than thin. Almost see-through.

In this land, the Japanese Ground Self-Defense Forces were nothing more than bugs in the Coalition of the Willing. Engineering ants and worker bees. They got the utilities up. Handed out medical supplies. Rebuilt hospitals and clinics.

They couldn't be trusted with anything bigger because they would go Empire on it and take over. That was the joke anyway. It was mistaken, but fair enough. It was the first time Japanese soldiers had stepped on non-native soil since World War Two.

So Japan drew the cush detail. Healthily supervised, of course. Not that Johnny minded. Samawah was just about the safest place in Iraq. No one he translated for let him forget it. He had already heard it three times from the Najaf-based Brits.

"Ban?"

Captain Cole was a short man with a thick neck, and a face like a boxer dog. He stood with arms crossed over his chest and his boots splayed wide, as if he planned on surfing an earthquake at any moment. His underbite hung pendulously as he awaited an answer.

Johnny swabbed sweat from his face for the forty-third time that day and said, "Yes, sir?"

"Kindly ask Takanori when he plans to have the grid operational in Sectors Two and Nine."

Johnny relayed the essence of the message, careful to insert his superior officer's omitted rank and remove the spiny tone. He then stepped back from the newly installed transformer and signaled for the nearest Private to lock it. The captain had seen all he had needed to see. It had been dead for weeks.

The new command post was to be moved further from the city center, half a click down the road. It was the only reason Captain Cole wanted to know. His superior had probably made an example of him, and now he was passing the favor on to Takanori. In any language, that was the military way.

"Why is he even asking?" Takanori had wispy hair and a wispier frame. He took a long drag on his cigarette, his face puckering like a dried-out pumpkin, before angling his chin down the street, at a husked building getting swarmed by a camouflaged construction crew. "The Americans have not delivered yet. He knows that. Is he trying to embarrass me, Sergeant?"

Takanori didn't actually want an answer. He was too busy removing his helmet and wiping his forehead with a handkerchief. Johnny liked him, even if he was from Tokyo and had gone to Waseda University. When he drank, which was often, the man called Harvard the Waseda of America.

Ban turned to Captain Cole. "That's unknown at present, sir. Right now it depends on receipt of the wiring."

Down the road, the pencil-thin dog leapt from the sidewalk to catch a lumpy ball. When he clamped down on it, the children shrieked all at once.

"And when is *that* supposed to be here?"

Ban translated the question. Takanori waved it away with his smoke.

"He thinks I can make wiring with my bare hands, Sergeant?" He shook his head. "Idiot!"

When the dog flopped down in a balcony shadow to lick its trophy, the kids couldn't resist poking at it, trying to free the ball while the knot of enlisted guns to Johnny's right scanned rooftops. Checked watches. Complained about tea. How it never tasted right down country.

"It was supposed to be in two weeks ago, sir." Johnny waited for that to sink in before dropping the words in that would make everything okay. "It's civilian-contracted to the Americans."

He watched the sentence hit its mark behind Cole's eyes and transform into redness on those hanging cheeks.

"Those bleeding bastards—"

Whatever else Captain Cole had to say, First Sergeant Johnny Ban never found out, because ten yards away, a black hole opened and swallowed them whole.

One second, First Sergeant Johnny Ban was there in the universe, in a very definite place on earth, in a country, in a city, and the next...

He wasn't.

He didn't hear the blast.

Didn't feel it.

He didn't come to, bleeding in the street.

The world simply opened, and his body disappeared.

When Johnny cracked a mudded eyelid, he was flat on his back in a helicopter, rising into the sky.

Something that looked like a face painted on a freckled balloon hovered over his. It had no ears to it, no neck, but it did have blue, oval eyes and a reddish grin the size of a tennis court.

"Hallelujah, brother!" It was a medic's voice. Loud. Coming through in Southern-fried English.

Johnny was in a neck brace, and couldn't smell anything but the scent of burning, and couldn't turn to see if Cole was next to him, or Takanori. Johnny had questions, about eight thousand of them, but his mouth wouldn't work no matter how hard he tried.

"You caught so much Fiat you're part-Italian now." The face drifted away for a moment, before sinking back down close to his. "Found a chunk of hood ornament in the wall, sticking out like a ninja star! How about that? Praise Jesus, brother. He sure put his hand on you."

Johnny tried hard to breathe, but a full-grown panther had plopped down on his chest, must have, because his vision streaked black as if a tail were swishing in his face, and he fought to wet his mouth so he could tell this to the balloon-man above him, but those blue eyes picked that very moment to float away.

ROOM 202

Johnny woke bone-tired, still wearing his clothes. He had wrestled off his jacket, one sock, one shoe, and his watch before getting pinned by sleep.

The nightstand clock read 2:03 a.m., yet a tangerine dawn had climbed in his window and painted itself up and down the walls of his new hotel room overlooking 1st Street.

Johnny worked aching fingers over too-tiny shoelaces until a familiar voice bullhorned into the room.

"Places!" It was Barry's voice, Barry with an A.

Johnny's fog-walk back to the hotel had been a slow one. His bad leg had seen to that.

He had to stop to gather himself in front of a seven-foot-tall cylindrical sculpture on Central that looked like people standing on the deck of a ship, or at least what a ship would have looked like if it were wrapped around a smokestack. He had run his fingers over the people etched in relief around its cold circumference. They were the first Japanese immigrants steaming for America, the *Issei*, memorialized in metal.

Shivering as he remembered it, Johnny sat himself up and leaned over to the window to crack the blinds.

"Want juice, man?" This voice was behind him, in the room.

Johnny's heart didn't ask permission to turn jackhammer before it went to work on his ribs. It just thumped him as he affected a yawn. He didn't turn around. "Couldn't sleep, Hector?"

"Had to check up. You looked bad last night. I asked for Asada this time and the desk jockey sent me up. Said you told her to send up everybody."

Johnny smirked. He had forgotten about that. "She gave you a key too?"

"Nah, I popped the lock when you didn't answer, and you can hate the invasion of privacy, or you can thank me for watching your back, because the people you have been playing with don't mess around, man. Just ask that dude at the sword shop."

Johnny rubbed his eyes.

"Thanks," he said, and he meant it. But all the same, he didn't want to know how long Hector had been sitting there, watching him sleep.

"Is that all you brought?" Hector nodded at Johnny's beaten-down suitcase flopped open on the floor. It looked like a split carcass. "Hey John, if I say something, do you promise not to take it personal?"

"It depends."

"I guess it does." Hector shifted where he sat. "All I'm saying is, you got a look like you don't let go of much. And you should. We don't have to take everything everyone tries to put on us. Not after Iraq, man. Just think about it."

Johnny changed the subject, asked about the early sunrise. Hector let him.

"The lead's dream sequence," he said. "Big effects shot."

His heartbeat near manageable, Johnny rubbed at a patch of drowsiness inside his forehead with the back of his hand. He couldn't reach it.

"The main character is a *Nisei* girl caught between two cultures. A little like you, John."

Johnny took the offered juice and raised the blinds to find that both sides of the street had acquired lines of cars while he had been sleeping. Tail-finned Caddies and flawless Fords sat on opposing curbs. Each side had a few cavities, but the row across the street was all black, and the near one, parked below his window, was all white.

The juice felt cold and good in Johnny's left hand, so he worked it over his knuckles before shimmying the window open with his palms to see that 1942 held his side of the street captive, gas lampposts and all, while the other side, that 21st-century present, hadn't changed. The Hotel Miyako shone tangerine, and the fire tower had gone blood orange.

In the middle of the street, clad in a gray nightgown, stood a girl who held herself like Emi Sato. She faced away from his window, but she had that same stooped-hurt posture as she straddled the street line. She looked out of place, this barefooted girl, like a *go*-piece on a chessboard.

"Okay, this side is America." Hector stood and waved a hand at where they were standing before pointing at the building across the way. "And that side is Japan, right? She's stuck between them, and, mythological things from both sides try to get her to choose if she's American or Japanese."

Hector went on about the folkloric figures on either side—Paul Bunyan versus a *tengu* and something else—but Johnny wasn't listening. He was too busy thinking about how this film knew enough to kick his hidden places whenever it wanted. But maybe that was what art did, he decided. Maybe that was what it was for.

"Roll one and two," the bullhorn screamed. "Action!"

The girl looked to the black cars first, then the white. She doubled over like someone about to vomit before wrenching first toward America, then Japan.

The bullhorn bellowed a cue, "Boom!"

She ducked too low, scraping a knee as Hector moved to the window and pressed his face to it. Just for Johnny, he interpreted the invisible. "That's a car flying over her head," he said. "They'll put it in later."

"Boom-boom!"

"That's our building exploding."

The girl spun and lost her balance, almost tumbled. She got up and ran.

Johnny held the sweating juice bottle to his other knuckles, flexed them, and immediately regretted it when a jolt of pain ripped up his wrist.

"Cut!" Barry's voice took what sounded to Johnny like a translation break before coming back in. "You need to *dance*. Do it like you're dancing! Violence is *style*. Again. Places!"

Johnny wondered if Keizo Kawari would agree with Barry's statement. He eyed the director's station, castled behind banks of monitors as tall as people.

"Silver doesn't shout. He delegates," Hector said, reading Johnny's mind. "That's real power. Folks like that don't *do* anything. They just plan it, then order it done."

Johnny palmed his lower back, ran stiff fingers over his kidneys, and remembered Oni's deadline.

THE DELEGATOR

It was late morning when Johnny woke. He didn't look at the clock. He only knew the sunlight outside his window was good and real.

Before making his bed with forty-five degree angles, Johnny downed his seizure meds with warm juice dregs. By the grace of medical science, he was free, maybe, for one more day.

Johnny's new room was the twin of his old one. Once-white walls had faded to a tea-stained, enamel-yellow. Rattling in loose screw sockets, a light and fan combo patrolled the ceiling at medium speed, twining its pullcords, threatening to take flight and plant itself in any wall at any moment.

Johnny took pity on the fixture. He knew how those spins felt. After all, Emi Sato was out there somewhere. And her dear departed father thought she was a monster.

Anchored to the wall opposite the bed and close enough to tickle his toes was a wardrobe that didn't quite headbutt the ceiling. It had full-length mirrors for doors though, and in them, Johnny watched a man who looked an awful like him prop himself up against a wood-veneered headboard and fight the potbellied reading lamp on the nightstand for a black phone.

The man with the rumpled face and the dark-circled eyes won, barely, and swollen fingers pressed the button to dial the only number in its memory.

When the ringing hit his ear, Johnny decided he liked making calls instead of being ambushed by them. He liked it a lot, actually. Enough to get used to it.

The line clicked in and Oni's voice slathered itself all over the connection.

"What a treat! I am so glad you rang."

Johnny held the phone a few millimeters from him. He ran a quick finger along the outer ridge of his phone ear.

"Speak to me," Oni said. "Tell me good things."

"Someone is following me. Is it one of your people?"

Oni was offended by the very suggestion, and let him know it with a series of tight little scoffs. One would've sold it. Three was two too many.

"A sword-vendor is dead. He gave me information on her before he died. Emi's father is dead too. The cops think he jumped." Johnny chewed the word. "Somebody pushed him."

"Fret not. Especially about Sato. The man was a money runner long before he tripped into public office. He drained the company bank account before running to America. Corruption charges are pending." Oni sounded pleased with himself. "The press got their bone, and they will gnaw it as long as they wish to."

"When I met him, he claimed his daughter had been kidnapped and that Kenji knew where she was. He tried to pay me one-fifth of a ransom."

One-fifth. Johnny had emphasized that part, and he let the implication zip over to Oni's Osaka office and hang around to spar with cat dander for two rolling seconds before picking the thread back up.

"So," he said, "who squeezed Sato?"

"Did you accept the money?"

Johnny repeated his question.

"Hold, please."

The line clicked. Clearly, something was happening on the other end that he wasn't allowed to listen to. Before Johnny had a chance to guess what it might be, Oni's voice came back like an icy road that encouraged one hell of a lot of caution.

"I hardly need tell you, Ban, that we are far from the only outfit looking for Emi. You assumed a certain level of risk in taking on this assignment, but is it not preferable to the alternative payment on your debt?"

"At this pace," Johnny said, "my body will hit the morgue faster than I can get a slot."

"You *are* tiresome." Oni cleared his throat. That simple act thawed the man's voice. The ice was gone and it took the road with it. It was only gravel now. "The Americans are after her, Ban. If we get to her first, we can protect her. If not..."

The implication wasn't lost on Johnny. "Which agency? Why do they want her?"

"Questions are wonderful, are they not? Such precious little things." It was the voice of a man used to delegating. "You have three days, Ban."

"Eight minus one equaled seven, last I checked."

Oni laughed like a father catching one of his children in an unintentional joke. He laughed so hard he had to stop and catch his breath before replying. And that was when the truth dropped on Johnny so matter-of-factly that every last gravelly pebble landed in his stomach lining.

"She will be dead long before then."

THE HALLWAY

The moment Johnny tapped his empty left-front pocket a second after the door closed and locked behind him, he knew it was going to be one of his bad days. They happened every so often and never with any warning. Days he put his underwear on backwards. Days he left the faucet running. Days he didn't put his medicine in his pocket — like this one.

It didn't help that Oni failed to give him any insight into the murders, or Emi either, for that matter. He decided not to take it personally. The man couldn't give a straight answer if he sold rulers for a living.

There was some good news. Sleep had banished the jetlag.

Johnny tapped his other front pocket. It crinkled. There were only two places left on the list: Nishi Temple, across Alameda on 1st, two blocks from his old Catholic school, and The Soft Spot, which also happened to be the place Keizo mentioned. That was the most promising.

It was a piano bar, and it wouldn't be open for hours yet, but Johnny could still stroll by it and get a sense of how it looked in the daylight, and where its exits were.

The hibiscus-girl was sitting in the little glass office, doing a crossword.

"Oh, hello," she said the moment she spotted him. "Did you see the blonde that was here for you?"

Blonde. She leaned on the word like she was jealous of it.

"No," Johnny said. "There must have been a mistake."

"I sent her up."

Johnny thought about the night he changed rooms. He had figured bad news had been waiting behind that door.

The opposite hadn't occurred to him.

Maybe the freckled flamingo had snuck up to his room to have a fling with the freak. She had been eyeing him. And it certainly wouldn't have been the first time. Occasionally his scars were good for something. Even if that something was curiosity-driven one-night stands.

Johnny smiled and said, "Blondes aren't my type."

"Oh," she said, looking simultaneously disappointed and heartened with that bit of information. "You have messages."

Two slips of white paper slid over the desk. The top one only had the name Rooney on it, and a phone number.

The bottom one was from Barry. It had two phone numbers and a statement. It said, *we need you at nine tonight.* Johnny sniffed and flipped back to the important one. He held the slip up so she could see Rooney's name.

"When did he call?"

"Less than an hour ago," she replied.

Johnny thanked her for the message, told her he had locked himself out of his room, and asked if she could please let him back in. He stepped aside when she smiled and jingled the master key at him.

But before she slipped by, she hit him with a theory or hers.

"You're looking for someone," she said. "Apparently, some-one not blonde."

Johnny massaged his aching knuckles. "Am I?"

"Telling me to send up anybody that asks for you kind of makes it obvious." The girl smoothed her flowers down. "Not that it matters, but you should keep looking. That is, if you're actually still looking."

Johnny didn't even have to ask why. He knew she would tell him eventually. It was shining in her brown eyes.

"I know I'd want someone to keep looking if he was looking for me."

She led the way back to his room after that, giving him a long look at her derriere in action. Up there, swaying on the stairs, it was cornucopia-full, but a certain tightness lingered in her hips, like she was ashamed of her own bounty, and that feeling had a funny way of knotting up in Johnny's chest with each step she took, depressing him, stair by stair, and it stuck to his ribs even after she had unlocked his door for him and gone away with the politest of nods.

He sat on the bed and thumbed his scars for a good minute after she left, and he dredged up memories of Emi Sato's vitiligo, of the pink spots on her face and neck and shoulders she had always hated—all the time wondering if any people, anywhere, loved their bodies. Especially the flaws.

ROOM 202

Rooney's line didn't even ring. It just clicked. When Johnny said hello and asked how the detective was feeling, he didn't get an answer. He got a question.

"Do you know a Johnny Ban?"

Ban. The detective had pronounced his last name like it prohibited something, not like it rhymed with *gone.* Johnny bit his lip. Of course, the man would only be asking the question if he had an idea about the answer.

"He's an associate of mine in Osaka." Johnny kept his tone even. Steady. "Why?"

"I got the decedent's daughter here asking after him."

Johnny felt his stomach shift. Decedent meant dead person last he checked. He had to clarify, so he asked if it was Mr. Sato.

"That's about right," Rooney said, and waited.

The man was good at waiting, and he wanted Johnny to know it too. He also wanted Johnny to hear the sob working the background like a low-flying plane.

Johnny's heart tussled up from his ribs and into his throat with incompetent rhythm, like the first time he learned the speed bag and missed every other sway.

Right this instant, right now, Emi Sato was sitting in that same sidecar Johnny had been in less than twenty-four hours ago. He swallowed, tried to rein his breath in. It didn't do any good. His heart was already up in his ears, beating them red.

"Are you asking if I'd be willing to put Miss Sato in touch with Mister Ban? Or is there something else?"

"Well, I'd appreciate it if you could take her off my hands," Rooney said. His palm grazed the microphone then, raising a hushed whisking sound. "She's obstinate and my translator can't get anything. Would you mind taking her to her hotel?"

"So this is a favor?"

The whisking sound came back.

"Yes," Rooney finally said. "I suppose it is."

"It's no problem," Johnny heard himself saying. He stretched his hand out, ran a finger down his forearm, and hooked it beneath his elbow crease just like a certain minnow on a certain Sato. He drew the scar there twice before stopping himself.

"There's just one more thing, Mister Asada. There was a homicide last night at the Little Tokyo Shopping Center."

"Really?" It sounded good to Johnny's ears, properly incredulous. He thought about the Rice King, about all that blood and cracked glass.

"Some karaoke owner," Rooney said as he flipped papers again. "Kawari."

Johnny almost dropped the receiver. Whoever had done it must have taken out the Rice King too, and maybe they only had time to dump one body...

Johnny forced words out as evenly as he could. "What happened?"

"Somebody poured him a beating, then chased it with a bullet. The L.A.P.D. doesn't appreciate bad news in Little Tokyo," Rooney growled. "It's our backyard, Mister Asada, and we always keep our backyard clean."

It sounded like a threat. Maybe it was.

THE LITTLE SISTER

What little buoyancy Johnny had left drained out of him when he saw the woman waiting outside police headquarters in the hot white noon. Even from a distance he could tell that the figure wrapped toes-to-neck in black wasn't Emi at all.

It was Hana, her little sister, pacing forth and back on coltish ankles.

Those legs of hers were too thin, her hips too narrow, and her shoulders tilted themselves high to one side like a bad shelf. She had a sharper chin than he remembered, and those eyes were nothing special, just a muddy brown. She framed them with crisp bangs though, and the rest of her hair graded away from her shoulder padded dress at a severe angle. It was a pretty black helmet all right. The kind that cost an awful lot of money.

She was alone out front, dragging her shadow around, but Johnny knew someone was keeping an eye on him from the inside. He could feel it through the mirror-glass. He kept his eyes on that as he approached.

He watched his blue reflection walk up to her and bow. She started when she saw him. It could have been any number of things that stopped her. His scars. His presence. Their history. All of the above.

"I am introducing myself because we have never met before." Johnny loaded his very formal Japanese with a tone not to be taken lightly, then bowed once more. "Please do the same."

She hesitated, but did. He gestured to the sidewalk as if offering it to her.

"Walk," he said.

Her high shoulder flexed as if she meant to argue, but he cut her off.

"Not here."

EDO CAFÉ

In a shaded café patio off Judge John Aliso Street, Johnny planted Hana in a green plastic chair and seated himself directly opposite. She didn't appreciate it, and he didn't much care.

This particular fenced-off patio accounted for only a small section of a larger red-bricked cobble that formed the courtyard of the old Union Church. It was a theatre now, or so the sign across from them said.

Twelfth Night opened next week. *All Asian Cast*, it said. Behind the marquee was a shiny new parking lot two stories tall, and the sun played over windshields and headlamps there, trying to find the right angle to glare in his face.

Johnny turned his head, showed her his good side.

"Why are you here?" Her voice played ice pick. It was kind enough to let him know he was the ice.

"You were asking for me. I figured you knew."

"Big words coming from a kidnapper." Hana took out a long-necked cigarette and put it in an ivory holder before lighting it. She must have thought it added a level of sophistication to her look. It didn't. It made it seem like she was trying too hard.

"Now, how would Hana Sato know to ask for me at the police station?"

She gave a tight smile at that, one that knew more than it let on. Far more.

"*There are no kidnappers.* You know there never were." Johnny raised his voice, up from its harsh whisper. "Maybe you put Kenji up to this? That makes sense if you wanted a cut. Or maybe Oni told you I was here. Maybe he wanted you to go to Rooney and ask about me, to put me on their map. There really is no better way to start framing me."

"You got any more maybes stashed away, Johnny?" Hana's tone dripped with annoyance. "I could put them in my piggy bank. Save them for a rainy day."

A curly-haired old woman came by with their order. Hot green tea for him. Iced coffee for her.

When she was gone, Johnny growled, "I need to know why your father sent Emi away."

A thin stream of smoke hit him in the chest.

"Will you tell me," she loaded her words with coiled frustration, one undisturbed by the years, "why *you* ran off all those years ago?"

Taking Hana's virginity two months after Emi disappeared hadn't been the best idea Johnny Ban ever had, but it helped that it hadn't been his. The girl had thrown herself at him. He just caught her. It had been stupid to go looking for Emi in her sister's body, but he did it, and all he found was that they weren't the same person. Not even close.

"When you enlist, you go where they say."

She blinked, stirred her coffee, and decided to answer his question, "You believed what you wanted to. And you were never family, Johnny. It was a private matter."

"Did she try to kill herself?"

Hana dodged that one. "Your face, how did that happen?"

"Change the subject again and I might have to shake some answers out of you."

Hana cut her eyes at him. "Promise?"

Johnny leaned forward and rephrased the question about Emi's suicide attempts. Hana leaned forward as well, to show him she wasn't impressed.

"Maybe," she trilled. "Who knows? Who cares?"

"Your father said she did."

"My father shipped her off because she *killed* Yuri. Remember Yuri, Johnny? That miserable, miserable girl?"

Johnny did remember. Yuri had had a big mouth and bigger fists. She had made Emi's life hell, teased her mercilessly about her vitiligo, even coined the term Yogurt Face. But she had been dead for years. Car accident.

"If it never occurred to you that Emi pushed her into traffic, you are *stupider* than I thought." She sipped at her coffee. "Everyone has to start somewhere."

"Start?" Johnny pushed his teacup back and forth on the tabletop, palm to palm. "Your father said an associate of his turned her into a monster."

"Come now, Johnny. You know the rumors."

He didn't. And his face showed it.

Hana liked that. She liked it very much. Any opportunity to make him squirm was worth basking in.

"Well, you do have an excuse. After all, being in the service can distance you a little, right?" Hana smiled into her coffee and played with the straw. She stared out across the street to where Parker Center was being demolished. "You always have been naive when it comes to her. Why, a grown man like you, having seen so much of the world, you know people kill for money. Some do it professionally. And I bet it would just sting you," she giggled around her words, high and loud and not even covering her mouth, "to know that *your* Emi is one of them."

Johnny fought for words. He didn't have any.

"I can be clearer," Hana said, twisting the knife and loving it. "My big sister is a *hired killer*. Emi kills for money, Johnny. It is her *job*. *That* is the monster my father referred to. That is what she became."

Johnny scoffed. Hard. He washed it down with a mouthful of too-hot tea. It didn't help.

"Grow up, Johnny! What you had with her is over." She put her eyes all over his scars. "Only piles of new hurts turn the old ones into joys."

Johnny did his best to fire back. "Who was this associate?"

Hana smiled at the remnants of Parker Center, as if the destruction on the other side of the street was something she felt personally proud of.

"Oh, Johnny, you are so cute."

"What did I say about changing the subject?"

Hana pulled a face, one full of faux innocence. "But you already *know* him."

Her drift caught Johnny between the eyes, and he knew the answer like he knew the ache in his kidneys.

"*Oni*," he said.

It made a cruel kind of sense. Connected two important dots. The word would've burned his tongue if the tea hadn't already taken care of that.

Hana didn't say yes. She just squealed.

It was enough to make Johnny use his last card. "I find it odd that you never asked how I knew what your father said."

Her gaze ticked over him, then away. It landed on the Union Church before fleeing to the sky.

"I met with him," Johnny said, "before he got pushed."

Her eyes were back on him now, and her shock seemed real. Her twitching mouth said so.

"I promised him I would get Emi back to her family."

"My father *jumped*." She was backpedalling now.

"He hit the pavement right in front of me, Hana. I looked up and saw someone run away as fast as he could."

Her small brown eyes got big in a hurry. He watched them turn into scales and start weighing things. Things she wouldn't tell.

"Fly back home," Johnny said. "Anyone who ever laid eyes on Emi is finding a way to drop dead in this city."

"I am *not* getting on a plane." Raising a curled hand, Hana weighed her bangs. She made a face like everything in the world was too heavy for her. "I have to ship my father home. Do you *know* how expensive that is?"

She put burning eyes on his scars and Johnny smiled the best hard-hearted smile he could muster.

"Do what you want," he replied, "just call someone else when you need help."

He felt his debt to her father coil in the air between them like a great cord, a towline tugging at the part of him that still remembered Mr. Sato's helpless eyes, those egg-knots of muscle working that jaw, and it got so tight between them that Johnny could hardly breathe.

He snapped it by getting up and walking away.

BULLY

When Johnny Ban first met Emi Sato, she was holding a garden hose dripping with blood. He remembered that much.

Cicadas ruled the Osaka summers of his school days. They came alive midway through his first trimester, weeks after he learned what *hafu* meant, what it felt like to have it whispered and shouted, what it felt like when it wormed around inside afterward.

Those cicadas never got tired of singing. *Min mi.* Even the Iraqi heat had felt incomplete somehow without them, and that was because heat was never just heat to Johnny. It had a sound. *Min, min mi.*

The name of that school was lost to him. The bomb tore it out of his brain, along with the name of the bully, but he remembered the bullying, the calloused hands, the face like a cinderblock.

Most of all, he remembered the water basin. The one that sat in the crooked elbow of a concrete hallway that led to the science building, the one next to the girl's bathroom.

Biology classes filled watering cans there, scrubbed beakers there. Art classes washed off palettes and left paint spatters on the metal that grew layer by layer over time.

It was a trough of a thing. It had five faucets and a basin deep enough to stack a class's worth of materials. Or shove a kid halfway in.

"Japan for the Japanese," the bully-boy had said while forcing Johnny under a spigot. He held Johnny's face up and grinned as he did it, showing too-small teeth the color of mortar.

Min mi.

Johnny cringed hard in anticipation of the water that would splash into his eyes, his mouth, his ears...

Spit dribbled down instead. It hit Johnny in the nostril and barged inside, smelling like garlic, chili, vinegar, as it rushed into his sinuses, into the back of his mouth. It tasted how it smelled.

Johnny coughed. But all that got him was a knock on the head from the nearest faucet.

The boy must have viewed the cough as a complaint, because the next thing Johnny knew, a soap bar was ramming itself against his teeth.

He jerked, spat. It didn't help any.

The grip stayed on his chin. The piercing alkali tang crawled inside his tongue. Bubbles frothed up at the corners of his mouth.

"Rabid mongrel." The boy wrenched Johnny out of the trough and onto the floor face-first. "Half-dog! Dogs like you should be put—"

He would have said more, but a harsh whistling sound cut the air, a swift scythe of a thing, one that ended with a whipping crack.

Johnny flinched and turned over. He scrambled to stand.

A horrible groan interrupted the cicadas then, and it surprised Johnny to learn that it came from his bully's mouth. And his bully wasn't standing anymore. He was on the ground.

A girl stood over him, a protectress, breathing heavy. She had the strangest marks on her face, an unwound hose in her hands, and a hall pass crumpled between her right palm and the scaly rubber. The thing looked like a great green snake with a metal mouth.

It whistled again when she brought it above her head and then down on the boy. On his ribs, his hands.

The boy screamed as she laced into him, ripping his shirt, bringing blood to his skin, pummeling his thighs.

She told him if ever did it again he would get it in the face next time, and then, she turned to Johnny.

"Hey," she said, "you want to hit him too?"

Johnny knew she was speaking to him, but he couldn't make out the words. He spat garlic and hung his head, but he kept his eyes on her.

Her face looked like a painting. Pink dots and white background. It looked like a patch of sky almost. Pink sunset clouds on her chin, on her ears.

Tiny circles of blood dotted her face. A thin constellation, they shone as the sun hit her skin. When she smiled, those clouds moved. They stretched out along her chin, gave way to the whitest teeth. All straight except for one turned incisor.

He recognized her. She was a grade higher, was one of the Sato sisters, the older one, the loner, and this girl held the hose out to him, blood ringing its copper nozzle.

Min, min mi.

Even the cicadas knew that for Johnny Ban, it was love at first sight.

CAPPERI

The Soft Spot hid a stone's throw from San Pedro and 2nd, on the third floor of a concrete building adorned with a metal grill starting on the second floor and ending at the roof. Spread out as they were, the metal slats looked like gap-toothed vertical blinds. Behind these, recessed windows peered down on the Federal Public Defender's office across the street.

At first, Johnny thought The Soft Spot wasn't there at all. A sign posted at head-height made it clear that something inside the building was leasable, and seeing as how the first floor was occupied, and the second floor was a Chinese restaurant, Johnny could only surmise that the sign referred to the unmarked third floor.

The street number matched the address the silver-haired lady at the hotel had given him.

Johnny surveyed the back of the building from a loading-zone alley that used to be Azusa Street. All he found was a city marker trumpeting that the Apostolic Faith Gospel Mission had birthed the Pentecostal movement there in 1906, excrement that was too big and grain-full to be a dog's, and that the club's front door was both the only way in, and the only way out.

It was also locked, video-surveilled by a half-orb of mirror-glass hanging from the entryway ceiling, and wedged against an Italian restaurant named Capperi that looked to be going out of business any minute. That is, if the long face manning the end of the bar was anything to go by.

Flanked by full bottles, the smallish man sat nursing a cup of coffee and moving his lips as he read his newspaper. He looked to be fifty, with busy brown hair waving in the wind of a lone fan and a distinctive unibrow that curled on either end like a moustache.

"Excuse me," Johnny said, skimming a bill from the brick in his breast pocket and cozying a Ben Franklin up to the man's coffee cup. "Would you happen to know the protocol for visiting The Soft Spot?"

The man dropped a finger on the article he had been reading, and his eyes came up tough, but when they hit Johnny's scars, they wavered. If anyone was in need of a soft spot, they seemed to decide after a fat second, it was Johnny.

"You call a number." The man had a voice like a rusty hinge. "Tell them Frank sent you. Just Frank. They give you an appointment, you show up on time, and there's a three-drink minimum. It's about as cheap as drinking diamonds."

"Is there another way in?"

The man tilted his head at him.

"Just the front," he said stiffly.

Another Ben Franklin surfed the newspaper. When a phone number came back in its place, it was Johnny's turn to do some pocketing. While he was in there, he pulled out the photo of Emi Sato.

"Have you seen her?"

The man took the photo of Emi and stared at it like it was a puzzle missing a few pieces. Pieces he had misplaced somewhere nearby.

"She's not one of the next-door girls, but she looks," he trailed off, then shook a finger at the photo. "I think she was here last night, well, for a drink anyway, before she went next door, but she doesn't look like this anymore."

Johnny twitched. "What does she look like?"

"For one thing, she's blonde." He stood up and leaned over the bar. "Real gold-blonde."

Johnny nodded for the man to go on.

"She's lighter than this. Pale as the inside of a coconut. I thought she was halfie, you know?"

Johnny knew, and he didn't know, all at the same time. But what was worse, his stomach was stomping his guts out.

It was the mention of blondness that did it, because it struck him that maybe Emi had visited his room at the New Tokyo Hotel the other night, that maybe she had been wearing a wig.

Johnny chiseled into the silence by thanking the man and asking him if he was the owner of the establishment.

The man smiled in a way that pained him, looked at Johnny's scars again, and reseated himself. He didn't pick up his paper. Instead, he stared over the chalky tablecloths in the place, tablecloths that hadn't needed to be changed in days. Johnny recognized that look.

He had seen it lurking in the bathroom mirror in his room above the bus station in Osaka. It was a face that didn't know how much longer it could hold out, or if it even wanted to. It was a face that didn't know what getting up from under, even for a moment, felt like.

"How much is rent on a place like this?"

The man grimaced at Johnny's question, and when he did, his singular eyebrow came down like a curtain over his eyes.

"Here?" The manager slung accusing hands at the walls. "Twenty-two hundred plus utilities."

Johnny shaved some paper off the brick Oni gave him as a going-away present, counting out twenty-three Franklins onto the bar before turning to go. If he had wanted to, he could have knocked the little man over with a cough.

"You're too good to be caught up with someone like her," the man finally said. His voice was thin, sucker-punched by shock.

It stopped Johnny at the door. "Caught up in what?"

"She's nothing special, this one. You got to let her drift. Rip that photo up. Move on. She'll drag you down, kick your guts so hard they come out your ears."

"Can't you tell?" Johnny smiled as he tugged an earlobe. "She already has."

NISHI TEMPLE

The temple building sat nearly flush to 1st, only a thin garden between stairs and street. With its gray tiled roofs and white walls shot through with brown timber, it looked like two temples huddled together for warmth.

Local sparrows hid their heads in its shaded places and chittered back and forth. Johnny didn't blame them. It was hot out. So hot he had taken his wet jacket off his wet shoulders five blocks back. So hot that his socks had gone flat in his shoes. The leather in the heels rubbed him wrong every step up the stairs.

There was an office inside, one sectioned off by walls with wide rectangular windows. Through the glass, Johnny saw an old woman, waited for her to finish talking on the phone, and stepped inside. She had kind eyes and didn't spend too long looking at his scars. When Johnny ran the photo by her, she apologized and touched her bobbed hair before saying she didn't recognize the woman, but oh my, was she pretty.

"But if you're willing to wait," she trailed off, eyeing a wall-mounted chalkboard that listed the days of the week, the hours of the day, and the names of the reverends assigned to the temple. "One of our ministers will be back shortly."

Johnny thanked her and killed time by browsing the main worship hall. Enough earth-heavy incense had tucked itself up in the nooks and crannies of the place that it would smell that way for as long as the building stood.

Apart from the hand-painted murals depicting the Buddha's life and times, the high-ceilinged worship hall had a distinctly American design. Rows of pews lined up on either side of a main aisle, which led to a stage bathed in yellow light. There was a large altar there, crowned with a golden Buddha, which Johnny supposed was beautiful in its way, but it wasn't his style. He took a seat halfway down the main aisle, squished his shirt against the cool wood, and closed his eyes.

He opened them when a gentle hand shook his shoulder.

"You look familiar somehow," the face above him said with a smile.

A long black robe marked the man as a reverend. He was stocky and topped off with salt-and-pepper hair. Besides a minor difference in nose-widths and chin-softness, the face in front of Johnny was an absolute replica of his old neighbor, Mr. Harada. Johnny asked him if he knew the man.

"I do," he said as he straightened. "Noriyuki?"

"He was always Mister Harada to me."

The voice sounded skeptical. "You knew him?"

"He taught me to pitch." Johnny hiked a thumb behind him. "Right there on Hewitt. I used to live over there with my mom."

"How?" Reverend Harada narrowed his eyes at Johnny for a moment before realizing it. "I'm sorry, what I mean to say is, you seem quite young, and I don't know how he could have taught you to pitch."

"This was over twenty years ago and he must have been in his seventies." Johnny said as he felt the reverend doing mental math to see if it added up. "I'm not trying to..."

"I'm Reverend Harada. Dale Harada." He blinked wet eyes at Johnny, took a handkerchief from the slacks beneath his robe, and sat down. "Noriyuki was my father. He passed last year."

He needed a moment, so Johnny gave it to him.

When Harada had collected himself, Johnny showed him Emi's picture, but he didn't know her, so Johnny changed the subject rather than answer questions about the man's father.

"How did you end up being a reverend here?"

"I've served other places, but I requested this posting. I suppose I felt as though I'd been called home."

Johnny hadn't meant for a question to come, but it did. "This is home for you?"

"Inasmuch as home can be outside this body, yes." He shrugged and let his shoulders fall. "You know, one thing they don't tell you about growing older is that you get tougher, and softer, at the same time. It's one of those simultaneous processes. They might even be in proportion to one another."

He laughed the laugh of a man who didn't take himself seriously.

"Of course, I practice not getting attached to things, that goes with the job, but all the same I find it easier to deal with difficulties because I've experienced them so often. And what do I mean by that? Well, I presided over eight cremations last week. One of them was a dear friend's. Did you ever know the Terasawas?"

Johnny shook his head. He didn't know the name.

"Well, I knew Stan since we were boys. He and I used to skip stones under the First Street Bridge, and pocket oranges from Missus Fukuda's fruit stand but you don't need to know that." He sighed a happy sigh, and eyed Johnny warmly. "Few Japanese-Americans know what it was like to grow up here. Not like you and I. After the camps, it was off to Gardena, to Torrance, but Little Tokyo will always be our spiritual home."

Reverend Harada shook his head. He smiled as he did, and the skin around his eyes wrinkled into well-worn paths.

"I performed the rituals for Stan as I would for anyone, and it didn't weigh on me. It was an honor. But when you told me my father taught you to pitch, something *hit* me." With his watch jiggling on his wrist, Reverend Harada's outstretched fingers sought his left-breast pocket and settled there. "I'm more able to deal with those difficulties, and less armored against unexpected moments, I suppose. Words, books, movies. These things sneak up on me now. They stir whatever most makes me human."

Reverend Harada laughed at that, but a trembling note got stuck in his throat. "This has all the makings of a dharma talk. What would my father think about me being so weepy, eh?"

The Reverend excused himself. He asked Johnny to come again, to share a pot of tea next time, and not to worry, to stay as long as he liked.

Johnny sat in the pew for a spell, soaking up the hush. When he had his fill, he walked out into the day.

The afternoon sky had fixed itself up like a layer of whipped cream spread thin over a blue bowl, and afternoon sunshine tinted white as it lit it through. The Gold Line train buzzed a warning as it passed. It was coming over-ground, and it advised pedestrians not to cross 1st Street.

Johnny timed sparrow races as they flitted from tree to tree, and he supervised two striped cats as they patrolled the front garden, gingerly avoiding fallen pine needles. When he tired of that, he crossed 1st on Vignes, and walked to Hewitt.

Standing in the street, Johnny stared at the window he had looked down from many years ago, when he had been only an American boy and knew nothing else but school, Mother's Japanese lessons, and baseball.

He gauged the distance from the light pole to the awning at 106. They were still four first-floor windows apart. For him and Mr. Harada, it had been the distance from the pitching mound to home, and he remembered, dimly, the way his lungs used to burn when he ran from one to the other and back.

HEWITT STREET

Past gleaming, earth-toned stacks of luxury apartments that looked like mismatched building blocks with balcony-rashes, Johnny dragged his soles down Hewitt, tapping pockets, wondering over the list Oni had given him.

Karaoke Weekend and Nishi Temple were done. Only the Soft Spot was left.

In two days, he hadn't learned much. He knew that Mr. Sato blamed himself for sending Emi away, and blamed Oni for what she became. He knew the Rice King thought she was pretty, and that Emi's picture drained Keizo's face to pale, which made more sense to Johnny now.

After all, Hana had taken a special pleasure in telling him her sister was a killer. He also knew Emi might be gold-blonde now, and that to a debt-drowned bar owner she looked like a coconut-colored halfie. Beyond that, people he talked to had a bad habit of dying or disappearing.

It still didn't add.

Between Hana's coincidental appearance at the police station and the timely death of Keizo Kawari, it looked to Johnny like he was easier to frame than a painting. They had taken his measurements the second the frog jumped him in that alley. Probably even before that. It was a good setup all right. The kind no one would question.

Kenji had known his name. Oni had too. They had known his background. He was targeted because they knew he knew Emi. Somehow. And Johnny didn't believe for a second that Oni wanted to protect her. Not from amorphous Americans, not from anything. In fact, it was entirely possible the opposite was true, that Oni wanted to hurt her. That Oni wanted her dead.

She had worked for the man, Mr. Sato had said so, and Hana had confirmed it, so Emi had fled Japan for a concrete reason. It was reasonable to assume that Oni was that reason.

Johnny took harder steps than he needed to, and his heels didn't like it, but he was too busy making up his own list to care.

It was a list of things Emi could have done that would've made Oni want to hurt her, that would have made her run. One, she had stolen something, either money or information. Two, she knew too much about something she wasn't supposed to. Or, on the chance Hana wasn't lying to him about Emi, there was number three. She had either killed someone she wasn't supposed to, or she had refused to follow through on a job Oni had given her. That was it, really. In Johnny's estimation, nothing else could have started this mess in Japan and dragged him in too.

But it still didn't make sense. She had never even been to Nishi Temple as far as Johnny could tell. The damn thing was probably on the list to keep him running around the edges of the real bad business, away from where he might see who was doing it, and away from helping Emi.

Yet through all the lies and half-truths, Johnny was still certain of one thing: the only reason he was a free man was because Emi was still alive.

She had to be.

If she wasn't, whoever had been following him and cleaning up on Mr. Sato, the Rice King, and Karaoke Keizo would have either killed him or dropped a dime and blamed him for everything. If that was the case, Rooney would have already been alerted that he was in the country under false pretenses, and after that it was downhill to the gas chamber, wrapped in a neat little bow.

A throbbing, regretful feeling settled into his stomach. Johnny knew he should have lied to Rooney when he had the chance. Telling him the truth about looking for an old girlfriend was the worst thing he ever could have said. It would contribute to motive when they found her body half-stuffed in a storm drain somewhere.

Of course he would be blamed for Emi's death when they finally got to her, and maybe that was the real reason why he had been handed a plane ticket and a stack of cash in the first place.

When she finally got it, Oni would hang it all on him. Every last bit. And why not? He was the obsessed ex. The one on medication. The one in the country under false pretenses. The vet with the scrambled head.

The papers would say she was running from him. They would say he was the monster. They would say he killed the others to get to her. It all made a sinking kind of sense. Johnny Ban was the perfect villain for this story, and, best of all, he had the face for it. A face fit for live news. A face you could instantly hate.

A flush surged to Johnny's cheeks. Oni was a genius.

Johnny flipped open the phone and pushed a button. Oni answered on the second ring.

"I know you set me up." Johnny tried to tone down the growl in his voice. He failed.

For three long seconds, all he could hear was purring on the other end of the line. Purring and mewling.

"If you want to live," Oni finally said, "call me when you know where the girl is."

"Who said I wanted to live?" Johnny smiled grimly, relishing the silence on the other end, the sound of Oni listening. Even he must've known that Johnny died years ago in that desert. Everything since had just been extra credit. "I will find Emi, I promise you that. But for my reasons. Not yours."

"I am so very *glad* we had this talk, Ban."

"Same here," Johnny said.

He heard laughter on the other end, high laughter, and then a click. Johnny didn't need to tell Oni that if Emi died he would be coming for him. There was never any sense in threatening people like that. They already knew the rules. Hell, they made them.

If Emi died and Johnny lived, well, Oni would have to spend what remained of his cat-loving life looking over his shoulder, because sooner than later Johnny would be there with a pair of plastic zip-cuffs and a pistol to do what needed to be done.

And with that vow set firmly in his mind, Johnny Ban did a very brave, and very stupid, thing. He threw Oni's phone in the nearest waste bin, turned on his heel, and since he was already on memory lane, he crossed the street to his old parish church.

It seemed a natural choice, what with his options dwindling. After all, there was no better place to pray.

ST. FRANCIS XAVIER CHAPEL

On the edge of the Toy District, the white sign for the Maryknoll Catholic School poked its head above a wall of juniper-lined fence. Behind it, three koi flags rippled on a pole above the center courtyard of the St. Francis Xavier Chapel complex: black, yellow, and green.

Johnny had picked a good day to visit the campus. Laughter-laced conversation peppered the air. Tag-playing children whooped and pounded out sprints on the asphalt.

When entering through the front gate, when passing by the bricked chapel administration building once painted white and now gone the color of old cottage cheese, Johnny Ban expected only a festival on this visit to his alma mater, not a breathing corpse. But there it was, right in front of him.

Standing back from the loose crowd, eating ice cream from a cup, it leaned against the garden fence, sunning its face. He hardly recognized it without the headband.

Johnny came up from behind and put a hard finger in the middle of the Rice King's forehead. Ice cream hit the asphalt and splattered as the dead man tried to run, but Johnny bent the corpse's wrist back like it was an hour hand. In the subtlest way possible, Johnny bent it to seven o'clock, and leaned against the fence too, shielding his tactic from any onlookers. The strangest thing happened then. The dead man felt pain.

Johnny kept his voice hard and cool. "What's your name?"

A dumb luck delivery of the highest order, the dead man blinked up at Johnny.

"I don't ask twice."

"Steven." The man shrunk two inches. "Steven J. Westlund."

"What brought you back from the dead, Steve?"

The answer came rapid-fire, almost like he had been waiting for someone to catch up with him. "I'm not supposed to be here. He told me to go, but it's my boy's kendo tournament."

Johnny cut him off. "That doesn't answer my question."

"A guy paid me five grand to smash my case and disappear."

"It was covered in blood, Steve."

"That was fake."

"Who put you up to it?"

Westlund gritted his teeth and scanned the courtyard.

"I," he stammered, "I don't know his name."

"What did he look like?" The question didn't get through to the man, so Johnny twisted his arm to eight o'clock, then to eight-fifteen.

The Rice King bit down hard on a scream.

"Like..." Westlund's watery eyes skimmed the crowd, searching for a word. "Like a *frog*."

Nearby conversations died in Johnny's ears.

Every last drop of saliva dried up in his mouth.

"How did it happen?" Johnny rasped the question. "Spell it out."

"He came to me an hour before you did. He waited in my back storeroom with a gun. After you left, he made me smash my case up and then hide in the back. Then he poured blood all over it. And, and when you guys came out, he snuck into the karaoke place. It was a practical joke, he said. Didn't seem like one. It seemed like a distraction. Something to get you out of there."

Johnny imagined frog-faced Kenji hiding there in the dark, staring out at him as he bought the steel knuckles. Imagined that face smiling the biggest smile ever smiled. Imagined that frog's finger on the trigger...

"You okay, Daddy?"

A pale boy with hazel eyes and sweat-mussed black hair stood not three feet from them, hugging a mesh-masked kendo helmet to his chest. When he didn't get an answer, he asked again. The kid was six years old, maybe, but he was *hafu* for certain. Johnny felt it in his bones.

"Daddy's fine, Mitchell."

Johnny exhaled sharply through his nose.

Westlund craned his neck. His eyes sought Johnny's. They were big, pleading things now.

"Don't," Westlund whispered. "He's my *world*."

The way he said it chipped Johnny's edges. It ran a crack through him. Head-to-toe.

"My friend is showing me a judo move, son." With his free hand, Westlund cuffed away loose tears. "It's good!"

A Japanese woman in a straw sunhat and a shapeless, tie-dyed dress appeared behind the boy. She placed two protective hands on his tiny shoulders.

"Leave town." A harsh whisper was all Johnny could manage. "Get them out of here."

Westlund nodded so hard he almost broke his own neck.

When Johnny released him, the man gasped and shot forward to wrap his son up in a one-armed hug while his clock-hand hung loose at his side. Watching Steven J. Westlund nuzzle his son's forehead shattered something in Johnny. Something small.

"No, Daddy," the little boy groaned, "I'm all sweaty!"

"Daddy has something special planned." Westlund tossed a furtive look at Johnny. "A vacation!"

The boy cheered at that, but the wife wasn't so easily moved. She kept her fingers knotted in the boy's loose black *gi*, and turned only as they turned, but she looked back after a few steps, eyeing Johnny like an old hawk.

He pointed his chin at the parking lot, and nodded at her to go. She squinted, thinning her lips out like she meant to say something. She didn't. She just went.

Changing direction with fabric-heavy snaps, the koi flapped their tails above Johnny, flying and sinking in the wind. In that courtyard, he tried to remember his own father. His chin. Or the way he walked.

Johnny got nothing. But the bomb wasn't to blame for it. It couldn't take out what had never been there in the first place.

Ensign James Wells had shipped out before his only son's first birthday. There had never been any vacations. No pictures either. His mother burned those.

It didn't stop Johnny from trying to conjure something up from his unconscious every now and again, especially when his lungs went concrete inside him, and the act of breathing wasn't much different from jackhammering a chunk of bad curb. Like now, for instance. This moment.

Of course, it didn't help Johnny's breathing that Kenji Asada was still alive, and worse yet, loose in Los Angeles. That was enough information for anyone to take in, much less the man who had apparently stabbed him to death in an Osaka alley just a few short days ago.

BRONZEVILLE

When Johnny got near his hotel, he found that the stretch of East 1st Street between Central and San Pedro had died and turned ghost town without a proper burial.

Lighting rigs had absconded. Classic cars, camera carts, and cranes were gone too. The wardrobe tent he had passed the day before sat partially collapsed at the end of the street, billowing against barricades like a giant, flattened spider.

There wasn't a soul left on the street.

High above Johnny's head, the sky busily dressed itself in dusk, but the street lamps hadn't tripped yet. White ropes of neon on the Chop Suey sign above the Far East Café hadn't either, and they wouldn't anytime soon, by the dark looks of things inside.

Wooden booths with high, stilt-thin frames sat square and solid in the middle of the room, a barrier between him and the back bar. On the walls, placed squarely between ornamented columns of dark wood, were black and white photos of the way Little Tokyo used to be. Pre-War. Pre-Internment.

Off to his left, the light greened on San Pedro. Traffic kicked itself and got going.

Johnny slipped a glance at the street before moving it back to the photos, wondering what the place had looked like after its residents had been ripped out, shipped to concentration camps.

He wondered how long the street stayed empty before black businessmen got themselves urged up Central to open jazz clubs and record stores in the vacant spaces, to turn the street into Bronzeville.

Mr. Harada had always liked that story, used to say he was glad someone was having fun while he was gone.

Hibiscus-girl was wearing hibiscuses again, and she had more messages for him at the front desk. Two were from Barry. He ignored those. The other was from Hector. *Shooting interiors in Geffen*, it said. *Don't go to that soft spot without me.*

Johnny was reading it for the second time, trying to figure out what the Geffen was, when he unlocked the door to his room and stepped in.

A cold gun barrel nuzzled up the two-inch, vertical scar on the back of his neck. Johnny pushed against it, barely, as he put his hands in the air. The thing was too thick to be a barrel.

It was a silencer.

REUNION

"My Johnny," Emi Sato's shocked whisper snuck over his shoulder and settled on his newly raised goosebumps. Her Japanese was heavy in her throat. "What did you do?"

For a hanging moment his heart didn't even want to beat. Then it mule-kicked him and almost broke two ribs. Stubborn and stupid and strong, it had wanted to stay there, in that moment when she called him hers.

Johnny wet his lips. The words had to be eked out.

"I played catch with a car."

It was true enough. The Fiat had fastballed him high, parts of it, anyway. So what if it wasn't being driven at the time, if it was thousands of tiny missiles instead?

She tapped the door closed behind him and snapped the lock. From her angle, she could only see his right profile, the pristine part of his face, and maybe she assumed the rest of him was whole too. Maybe.

She frisked him one-handed and apologized for it. As soon as she was done, the silencer broke off from his neck.

"This is my fault," she said.

This. It was an octopus of a word, one with arms enough to mean everything around him, everything that brought him to Los Angeles.

"Are you going to turn the light on," Johnny said, "or should we stand here all night not looking at each other?"

Of all moments, the street neon picked that one to jump whitely into the room. In for two seconds, then out for six, then in again—like a photoflash on repeat.

"If it will make you less shy, we could get married," he said. "We could have a cute little three-quarter-Japanese baby boy. We could name him Leonard and make him learn kendo."

Behind him, he heard Emi flinch. He dropped his hands and turned. Nice and slow.

Neon lit Emi's dark athletic shoes and sweatpants that made the most out of her runner's legs. She had certainly filled in. She looked like a gymnast now, and not even her loose, hooded windbreaker could hide the definition in her shoulders. His shadow was on her face, so he stepped to the side.

"I *am* married, Johnny."

He was about to say that was precisely what divorces were for, but when the neon snuck back in, he swallowed it whole. The woman standing before him was Emi, and it wasn't.

The Capperi barman had been right. She *was* blonde now, gold-blonde, but that wasn't the worst of it.

Her skin had been bleached to a ghostly pallor. The skin condition she had been born with had been burned right off her face. The map he had so often traced with his fingers was no more.

The pink continents once marking her chin, her ears, her neck, had been frozen over. She was all glacier now, from her forehead to her collarbones, and the generic smoothness shared by every member of the plastic surgery brigade held tightly to her new skin. She was a copy of a person now, with a real one trapped behind her eyes.

Of course, those had been cut too. Lids had been chopped and separated in every effort to remove their Asianness, to make her look European, and Johnny supposed it was good work if one didn't know the original, because what stood before him looked like a doll whittled within an inch of its life, and the sneer on his face must have told her so.

"I had to do it," she said. "To *disappear*."

Her left hand didn't know what to do with itself. Fingers flexed, folded. The rock on her ring finger, the one keeping a gold band company, was as big as a baby's eyeball.

Johnny needed the pieces to fit. "Because of Oni?"

Emi had a thick-gripped, subcompact pistol in her right hand. It was a front-heavy 9mm, sporting a snub-silencer, and what looked like a combo flashlight/laser-sight mounted beneath the barrel. Near her feet, a red dot hovered over the carpet like a scavenging insect.

It was good gear. The best. It was the kind of thing that confirmed what Hana had told him: Emi was indeed a professional killer.

And in this light, Johnny knew the old Emi was gone for good. The one who wanted to protect everyone but herself had fled with her continents. This truth torpedoed his stomach out from under him, rolled his gut over into a sad sinking thing.

He had missed too many years of her life to have any claim on her now. But he wasn't too late for what was left. For what could be. And that was something.

Her left hand gave up trying to wrestle itself and made straight for his face. Tentative fingertips poked coolly at each scar, dimpling his cheek, testing the glossy reality of his disfigurement.

"Careful," he said. "Might be contagious."

Emi stepped nearer, brought her new face to his, and where she went, the bright insect followed.

Her skin looked worse up close, where there were two red pinch-marks under her jaw, but up close, she smelled like flowery soap, and she kissed every scar of his that she could get her lips on.

Through her barrage, he said, "Your father thinks Oni made you this way."

Emi pulled back. Her eyes changed. Something got tight behind them, and she smiled a smile that looked like it hurt. At least her lips hadn't gotten chopped. Those were still the same. They curled up the same. But they didn't feel the same anymore, didn't slap like they used to. They prowled.

"Help me figure this out. Oni was your boss. You took important files from him." Johnny was grasping and Emi let him. "Then you ran to America."

"The less you know, the better, Johnny."

"Or he wanted you to kill someone and you refused."

She sniffed at that.

"You killed someone?"

Emi didn't have an answer for that one. The neon leapt right into the room, and leapt right out, but her face had changed in that time, and Johnny knew he was getting closer to the truth.

"Accidentally? Someone innocent?"

"No, Johnny, I did it on purpose. Oni paid me. He just neglected to say why." Emi's shoulders sagged. "You know, we could have had this reunion much sooner if you had stayed in your old room."

Reunion. The word hit him below the belt. Emi had been the blonde the hibiscus-girl mentioned all right. Not the make-up artist. Not the flamingo. And now Johnny's stomach burned at the confirmation that they had been only a door away from each other when he walked away and asked for different accommodations.

"So why come now?"

"It eats you up, Johnny. This work." She swung her hand in front of her face, and pulled a strand of blonde hair over her ear. "My fate was sealed the second I took that shot. My life is done."

Johnny flinched. It didn't take a psychologist to see that her work had broken her, again and again. He could tell she had nothing left to put herself back together. No glue in the universe could do it. Not this time.

He said, "There has to be a way."

"Be serious, Johnny. There stopped being a way a long time ago. All I can do is tie up my last loose ends."

Johnny dropped his gaze to the gun. But the red insect jumped then, offended by the implication that she had brought it for anything other than his protection.

"When I heard you were here," she said, "I knew I had to see you one more time, had to look at you and see the person I used to be, the person you remembered."

Emi was every bit the jawbreaker she once was, but there was something else in her face now, and the neon kept finding it. She looked fragile around the eyes, as if her hard edges had grown brittle with time, as if they might crack at any moment. "I have to make certain you get out of this alive."

"Emi." It was soft the way he said it, furtive, like he had been meaning to say her name that way his whole adult life, and maybe he had, because Johnny's heart pounded up in his throat now, and then it was in his mouth, on his tongue, spitting out words. "Did you ever think about me?"

Before she could answer, a focused explosion blew the doorknob clean off the door.

Ryan Gattis is a writer, curator, and creative writing professor at Chapman University. He holds an M.A. in Fiction Writing from the University of East Anglia in Norwich, England, and is the author of novels *Roo Kickkick & the Big Bad Blimp* and *Kung Fu High School*, which was acquired by The Weinstein Company. In 2012, he wrote and curated the story-driven art show "The Art of Kung Fu: Myths and Legends" and works closely with street art collective UGLAR (uglarworks.com) as Narrative Director on various public art projects. Raised in Colorado, he lives in Downtown Los Angeles.

Carmen Harbour is currently working as a freelance editor, writing on several short story projects, and is a contributing writer at online magazine Little Pink Book in Atlanta, where she currently resides. When not pushing red pencils, she likes to sleep (a lot) and watch movies (a lot).

Mark Smith (marksmithillustration.com) is a freelance illustrator and occasionally lectures on the BA Illustration course at Plymouth University in England. He has worked for magazines, newspapers and publishers around the world, including Penguin Books, Simon and Schuster, Hachette, The Folio Society, The Financial Times, The New York Times, The New Yorker, The Guardian, The Times, The Washington Post, ESPN, and many more. His images have also won recognition from the New York Society of Illustrators, LA Society of Illustrators, Communication Arts, 3X3 Pro Show, Association Of Illustrators, American Illustration, Creative Quarterly, and Creativity International. When he's not working, Mark likes to improve his throwing technique by throwing a ball for his dog Oscar who never, ever retrieves it.

BLACK HILL PRESS
Contemporary American Novellas
blackhillpress.com

Black Hill Press is a publishing collective founded on collaboration. Our growing family of writers and artists are dedicated to the novella—a distinctive, often overlooked literary form that offers the focus of a short story and the scope of a novel. We believe a great story is never defined by its length.

Annually, our independent press produces four quarterly collections of Contemporary American Novellas. Books are available in both print and digital formats, online and in your local bookstore, library, museum, university gift shop, and selected specialty accounts. Discounts are available for book clubs and teachers.

facebook.com/blackhillpress
flickr.com/ blackhillpress
instagram.com/blackhillpress
pinterest.com/ blackhillpress
twitter.com/ blackhillpress
vimeo.com/ blackhillpress
youtube.com/ blackhillpress

7505520R00074

Made in the USA
San Bernardino, CA
08 January 2014